The Fallen

Danielle Paquette-Harvey

1984 –

Cover by Danielle Paquette-Harvey

ISBN 978-1-998458-03-5

First Edition: September 2022

Published by: Danielle Paquette-Harvey

http://daniellephauthor.com

https://www.instagram.com/daniellephauthor

Subscribe to my mailing list so you don't miss anything!

daniellephauthor.com

Follow me

- Facebook: Danielle Paquette-Harvey author
- Instagram: daniellephauthor

Other books by the author

All my books are available on Amazon, in most libraries Barn & Nobles, and other good libraries.

Prequel to this series

- The prophecy *- ISBN 978-1777572105*

Origins

- The Goddess's Wards *- ISBN 978-1-7782178-8-3*

Longing mates Series

1. Age-Old Enemies *- ISBN 978-1777572136*
2. A Beloved Sin *- ISBN 978-1777572150*
3. The Fallen *- ISBN 978-1-7782178-5-2*

Blood and Kisses Series
    1. Cursed King – 978-1-7388313-2-6
    2. The Awakening – coming soon

Half-angel's daughter Series
    1. Devoured by Darkness – coming soon

Charity books

   •   A Wicked Taste of Fate – An Anthology -
       ISBN 978-1-7782178-6-9

       Please note: This dark fantasy anthology
       book contains eight short stories from dif-
       ferent authors. All the profits go to Ste-Jus-
       tine's, a children's hospital in Montreal.

Y'vagroth
Naiad Shrine
Moon Elve's Lands
Moon Goddess Shrine
Cabin
Leila's Pack
Montreal
Melian Nymph Sacred Grove
St-Lawrence River
Sam's Pack
Sleeping Lake
Chalet
Ancient Pack Ruins
Eurynomos Sepulcher

Darton's Castle
Delos
Mytvathyr
Valley of Nysa
Nokorath Hills
Vampire's Castle

Danielle Paquette-Harvey

The Fallen

Contents

Chapter 1 (Will)

A New Journey

The orcs barged into the room. The dragons tried to defend us, attacking the offenders and shielding us with their bodies. Rocks fell from the ceiling. But I didn't care. Her skin felt so cold, yet I didn't want to leave her. Damien got off his dragon and forced me to put down Leila's body on the floor. He was talking to me, screaming over the sound of the orcs. I didn't hear anything. I stared at her lifeless body. How I yearned to kiss those delicate lips! I couldn't live without her. My wolf was howling in pain. The mate bond was broken. It was torturing me. My heart was shattered. I felt sick to my stomach.

An axe swung right past my face. I turned around just in time to see Damien fight back an orc warrior.

"Come on, Will! We need to go!" screamed Damien after killing the orc. He climbed back on his white dragon and motioned for me to do the same.

He flew away through the hole in the ceiling, along with the others. I was now alone with Ladon and my beloved Leila: my treasure, my everything. The sacred sword was still lodged in her chest. Blood tainted her clothes, as well as my hands.

The orcs were fiercely attacking now. Ladon was defending me, but he would soon be overrun. Should I let myself be killed? What was the point of living if I couldn't be with the woman I loved?

My wolf snarled at me. He was right. Leila wouldn't want us to sacrifice ourselves just like that. She sacrificed herself to help us fight the demon. If I were to die, it would mean her death was for nothing. Anger burst in my chest.

I removed the sacred sword from Leila's chest just in time to parry the club of an orc. Droplets of sweat and drool from the orc splashed onto my face. The grotesque creature seemed surprised by my strength.

"I will not die, today!" I screamed in rage.

Thinking of Leila gave me strength. I was suddenly filled with an urge to live. I wouldn't let her death go to waste.

I crouched down and swung the blade of the sword upward, slicing off the orc's arm. A cry of pain echoed from the creature, overshadowing all other sounds. The arm fell heavily on the floor, the club still clutched in its hand. A loud clang resonated in the room as the blunt weapon hit the floor. The arm slightly bounced on the floor and a piece of muscle separated from it, falling a little further. The room fell silent. Everyone was staring at the lifeless arm, lying in a pool of blood.

I didn't wait for them to snap out of it. I climbed onto Ladon's back.

"I'm so sorry for leaving you," I whispered to Leila as we flew away through the hole in the ceiling. Tears rolled down my cheeks. I clenched my teeth, trying to push away the pain and sadness, leaving room only for anger in my heart.

The others were waiting for me on their dragons.

"Quick!" stated Damien, "We need to get back to the castle. Bianca is waiting for us."

I flew right past them. I knew exactly where I wanted to go.

Damien shouted at me, "Where are you going? The castle is south, not west."

"This bastard took her away from me. I will take his life with my own hands."

I didn't wait for them to answer anything. I wouldn't let anyone try to stop me. I kept flying west, watching the dark landscape of November. Nature looked as dead as my sweet Leila.

*********** Blake's POV ***********

I watched in shock as Will flew away on his dragon. Cara cried, trying to get her lover's attention, but Ladon didn't look back. Will's wolf was his Alpha. He would follow his lead to the end of the world, despite his love for Cara.

"Stop him!" Ravynne shouted. "He's going to get himself killed."

I knew she was right, but I also knew Will. He was an Alpha. He had the soul of a warrior. Nothing would stop him. The mate bond was broken, leaving a wound inside his heart that would never heal. I looked at Damien. Since he was my vampire Lord, I would go if he ordered me to.

"No," Damien answered.

He was calm, and his voice inspired respect and authority.

"Let him be. He chose his destiny. Let us return to the castle together."

I nodded to him. Ravynne took one last look at Will, then followed us.

We flew south towards the vampires' castle. Everywhere I looked, it seemed the demon's army was swarming. They were destroying farms and attacking villagers. The people were overrun. Flying enemies were getting out of our way since our dragons inspired fear and respect. They wouldn't dare confront us. Even the harpies stayed away.

"We should help them!" I shouted at Damien.

He turned his head towards me.

"We don't have time for this. We need to concentrate on the demon."

I nodded. He was right. But my dragon was young and full of pride. Like me, he felt an urge to help. He wanted to fight the enemy. He breathed fire at enemies that were close enough. I watched with satisfaction at the goblin's flying machines catching fire. The panicking goblin would come crashing down in his machine before being crushed upon impact. If I was lucky, bonus damage was done to the enemies on the ground at the same time.

We continued south, flying over the Valley of Nysa. The nymphs were fighting fiercely. Seen from above, their magic was creating a beautiful display of color. I hoped they would be victorious in their battle against the demon's army. No matter how strongly I wanted to help them, I knew the enemies would continue flowing if we didn't deal with the demon. Damien was right. He was a good and wise Lord. I was proud to be able to serve under his rule.

Soon, the castle came into view. I was shocked by what I saw. Enemies swarming everywhere around the castle, pounding at the door. The main gate had been breached. Our soldiers were still battling against the enemy, but many of them appeared to be wounded.

On the floor, piles of corpses were laid out. The odor of blood could be smelled all the way through the air. Whatever happened while we were away? I thought our army was strong enough to protect the castle. I looked at Damien. His jaw was clenched. I could understand his worries. The Queen was in the castle. I hoped she was safe. "Let's get them!" ordered Damien.

Ravynne's dragon was old. He stayed in the air to fight off flying goblins. Ravynne started to cast spells. Her witches' powers were strong enough to attack the ground from the sky. The two of them made a great team.

Clara started spitting white energy bolts, stabbing enemies from the air. I was amazed by her speed and agility.

Damien and I dived to the ground. Our dragons were leaving trails of fire, stopping the advance of the demon's army. The screams of the orcs catching fire and the smell of burned skin were delectable.

I laughed as I reached the ground and got off my dragon. I picked up a sword on the ground and started slashing through enemies. I had been craving battle for a while. Nothing could beat the sound of an enemy dying.

I heard a noise and turned just in time to see Damien biting off flesh from one of the creatures. He was slashing with his nails, dismembering them. I guess the fear of losing his mate was making him desperately dangerous. In one big pound of his feet on the ground, he sent a shock-wave of energy that got everyone down. I had forgotten how strong the vampire Lord was.
Quickly, I got to my feet and started killing as many enemies as possible while they were still startled. With the help of the dragons, we managed to kill all the remaining creatures.

Panting, I let my sword fall to the ground. I was dirty, bloody, and sweaty, but I felt great. It'd been a while since I had a good workout. Satisfaction filled me when I looked at the corpses on the ground.

Behind us, the castle's doors opened. I turned around to see Kate running towards Damien.
"Damien!" she cried as she fell into his arms.

She didn't care that he was dirty and full of blood, the joy of seeing him filled her. He hugged her tightly, lifting her from the ground while they kissed.

"Why didn't you tell me how bad things were?" he shouted at her, before adding more softly, "Something could have happened to you and the baby…"

His last words were a whisper. The thought of losing his wife and baby was eating his soul.

Hearing them talk felt like I was prying into a secret I wasn't meant to hear.

I turned my head around to see Bianca running out of the castle.

She was smiling happily, shouting to us, "You did it! You broke the curse!"

She stopped and frowned when she scanned around, suddenly realizing.

"Where's Will? Where's Leila?"

I exchanged a look with Ravynne. "Let's get inside," suggested Damien. We all nodded and followed his lead.

"Get the wounded inside the castle," ordered, Kate. "Get them to the ballroom. We'll set up an infirmary there. Elwin will heal them."

Soldiers started to help the wounded ones get to the castle.

"I can help too," offered Ravynne.

"Great! Go meet with Elwin," replied Kate. She motioned to the soldiers.

"The main gate needs to be repaired. We need to build fortifications. There will be more waves to come. All who are not wounded must prepare for the next wave." Everyone got busy. The dragons made it clear they were staying to defend the castle as well.

Damien put his arms lovingly around his wife's hips. "It was a great decision to leave the castles in your hands. You are a great queen, my love." He flashed her a smile as they walked to the castle.

I felt happy for their love, but this wasn't for me. I never was a romantic one. The only thing I enjoyed was fighting. That's all I ever had in my life. Giving myself up in battle until my body wanted to give from under me. The rush of battle, knowing that only one of us will survive the battle. *That* was what made my heart beat faster.

The inside of the castle was as beautiful as ever. No signs of battle could be seen. The marble was intact, as well as the statues and embroidery. The only thing that betrayed the war that had raged outside was the wounded soldiers getting to the ballroom. Ravynne met with Elwin inside the ballroom and helped tend to the wounded.

I followed Bianca, Kate, and Damien to the throne room. Steven embraced Bianca as she entered the room. Arius was there, along with an elven woman I had never seen. It looked like fate had given him a second chance at love. I smirked. It was nice to see my friend so happy. All this showcasing of affection was getting under my skin. What did I do to be surrounded by couples? I longed for the moment I could get back to the battlefield.

"Now that we're here, won't you tell me where Will and Leila are?" asked Bianca.
I waited for Damien to speak. He was the lord; it was his place to say it.

"Leila is dead," he said calmly.

Bianca and Kate gasped. The room went silent, everyone waiting for his explanation. "In order to break the curse, she had to be sacrificed… She was the beloved treasure in the riddle."

"She died… because of me," whispered Bianca, silent tears dripping on her cheeks. Kate was crying silently in Damien's arms.

This was wrong. Leila wouldn't have wanted this.

"It was her destiny," I replied with a strong voice. They all turned towards me as I continued.

"Leila had been destined to be sacrificed since the night she was born. She bore a mark on her neck. Passed down from one generation to another, throughout the history of her pack. She knew what needed to be done, and she accepted her fate."

"It doesn't make it easier," sniffled Bianca.

Damien answered gently, "I know, but she sacrificed herself for us to be able to fight the demon. We can't let her down."

He was right. If we didn't want her sacrifice to be for nothing, we needed to go after the demon. Everyone nodded.

"But then, where's Will?" asked Bianca with a small voice.

Damien sighed, looking at the floor. "After the death of Leila, he flew away on his dragon, swearing he would take the life of Eurynomos."

"No!" shouted Bianca. "I'm the Moon Goddess's daughter! It's my duty to do this. He won't be able to do it."

I cursed to myself. I had feared as much. That it was somehow related to the Moon Goddess. But it was too late. He was gone already.

"We couldn't stop him. He chose his fate," answered, Damien.

Doubt crept into my mind. We didn't even try. Maybe we could have caught up with him if we tried? Was it too late? Could we still find him if we went now?

"Let's make sure we're prepared for the next wave," Kate answered softly. "Then we'll prepare our next plan of action."

She did make a fine Queen even though she wasn't a vampire. Will was her brother too, but she composed herself better than her sister Bianca. She really was a worthy mate for our vampire Lord.

"I will help with the archers' preparations," said the elven woman. "Thank you, Elashor," answered Kate. Arius grabbed Elashor's hand and kissed her lovingly before letting her go. I smiled at him. "It's nice to see you happy again." He chuckled lowly, "Thanks, Blake." I exited the room. The earlier battles had left my clothes tainted with my enemies' blood. I was dirty. A warm shower will feel amazing. I wouldn't say no to eating a proper meal either.

*********** Bianca's POV ************

People got busy with the repairs to the castle. The sound of hammers and people talking filled the room. It was as if nothing happened. I felt crushed. Leila had been killed because of me. How could I ever live with myself again? I never wanted for anyone to die. Now, because of me, my brother lost his mate. Would he hate me? Would he ever speak to me again? We didn't even know where he was. He went on to kill the demon by himself. The demon that *I* was destined to face. I didn't want to have his death on my shoulders too. My hands began to shake. I couldn't hold my tears in. I felt so guilty about what had happened.

"Hey!" I turned around. My sweet Steven was there, smiling gently at me. His blond hairs were messy, but I thought he looked sexy that way. I wiped the tears from my cheeks.
"Steven."

He wrapped his strong arms around me. The warmth of his body was soothing my pain.
He whispered gently, "Stop blaming yourself."
"How did you?"
"Did you forget you're my mate?" he asked with a smirk. "I can hear your thoughts if you leave the link open."

I felt embarrassed. In the heat of emotions, I had completely forgotten.
"But I'm happy you did," he continued, before kissing me on the lips. "Or else I wouldn't have heard your sadness. You would have stayed alone, to bear all those thoughts by yourself."
I rested my head on his chest, listening to his heart.

"But it is true…"

"No, it's not! Everyone was aware of the dangers when they embarked on this adventure. If anyone is responsible, then let it be Eurynomos."

Was he right? Could I truly believe I wasn't responsible for Leila's death? I looked up into his eyes, searching for an answer. His blue eyes were full of conviction.

"Thanks, I'll try to stop blaming myself."

I forced myself to smile. Steven grinned.

"I'll keep watching you. I'll say it to you as many times as you need to hear it. I will continue until you stop blaming yourself."

I giggled. Steven was so sweet. I was blessed to have such a great mate.

"Do you even know how much I love you?"

He smiled and grabbed my chin with his hand.

"Oh yes, I do!" he whispered before kissing me.

His kiss made all my worries go away. My heart started beating faster as our tongues danced together. I opened my eyes slowly as we broke the kiss.

We walked to one of the balconies. The repairs were well under way. Lilith and Zach were giving orders. Soldiers and workers were following their orders, giving us a chance to be ready when the next wave would hit us. Elashor was preparing the archers, giving them tips to avoid being hurt by the enemies. Even Blake was there, sharpening swords and making sure all the weapons were in good shape. But what amazed me the most were the dragons. It felt unreal to see those four big dragons resting in the courtyard. I had never seen such powerful creatures. To think they were ready to protect the castle against the demon's army was reassuring.

Steven gave a low, long whistle of admiration as he leaned on the railing.

He asked me, "Majestic, aren't they?"

"Yes, they are! I didn't even know dragons existed."

"Me neither."

"I wonder how their skin feels to the touch."

These legendary creatures felt unreal. I wondered if they'd let me touch them. Would dragons enjoy being pet?

Steven pondered before answering, "I guess they feel like a lizard."

I nodded. I was disappointed, but he was right. Somehow, I liked to imagine they were fluffy and soft. But they had scales on their backs. It wouldn't be like petting a kitten.

He added, "Blake says that Will's dragon had six heads."

"Wow!" I exclaimed. "That must be an amazing sight!"

"Hopefully, we'll be able to see him when Will joins us again."

"Do you think... he'll come back to the castle?"

Steven shrugged his shoulders. "Maybe."

I would be overjoyed if Will came back to the castle with us.

"I hope so," I whispered.

He turned to me, as if suddenly remembering something.

"Well, now that the curse is broken, shouldn't we prepare to go deal with this demon?"

I nodded to him. "Yes, but I'm not sure how to do it."

"You told me that you felt your magic power grow when the curse was broken, right?"
I nodded again. It was true. A surge of magic power filled me when the curse with the demon was broken. I felt so powerful.

"Yes, but I have no idea how to use this magic."

Steven held his chin while thinking. "Why don't we ask Elwin and Ravynne? Ravynne's a witch, and Elwin has been the castle's sorcerer for centuries! Surely, one of them would know?"

I nodded, excited. "Yes! That's a great idea!"

We hurried back inside to the ballroom. The room looked nothing like the last time I was there. Dozens of wounded soldiers were laid out on stretchers. It smelled like alcohol and disinfectant. Elwin had brought a workbench on one side of the room. He would mix the correct ingredients on his workbench, adjusting them to the needs of the person he was healing. Then he would bring the prepared potion to his patient. On the other side of the room, Ravynne was reciting spells, a white wind swarming around her as she healed the wounded. Elwin's potions took some time to completely heal, but Ravynne's spells were instantaneous. We were so lucky to have such a powerful witch with us.

"Elwin!" I shouted, as I ran to him.
He dropped the potion he was working on and turned to me.
"What is it, my Lady? I'm rather busy right now."
"I know. I need your help."
"How can I help you?"
"Well, you see, since the demon's curse has been broken, I have regained my powers. But I have no idea how to use them."

Ravynne joined us while we were talking. She commented, "Learning to control your powers will be critical in our fight against the demon."
"I know, that's why I've come to see Elwin, or you, Ravynne. Do you guys have any idea how I could learn to use them?"
Elwin was passing a hand in his hair as he thought. Ravynne replied, "I only know how to teach witches magic. Even if that could prove useful to you, it would take months to master it. I'm afraid we don't have time for this."
I nodded to her.
"I know!" exclaimed Elwin, before continuing, "You should head to Mytvathyr. It's the biggest elven city, far to the east."
"Mytvathyr?" Asked Ravynne. "I've never heard of it."
Elwin's eyes sparkled, and a smile appeared on his face as he spoke with passion.
"It's home to the most ancient magic guild of these lands. The leaders are high elves, renowned for

their great magic knowledge. I studied there when I was still a young vampire. If anyone can teach you, it's them."

Ravynne looked like she was impressed by his knowledge.

"This sounds like a great idea!" I exclaimed. "Let's find Kate and Damien. We need to tell them about this."

I left the room with Steven while Ravynne was still talking lively with Elwin.

We got to the throne room and explained everything to Kate and Damien. They called for everyone to join us in the strategic room. A big wooden desk filled the room with chairs all around it. A large map was displayed on the desk, letting us see where Mytvathyr was situated. No roads led to the city; we would need to go by horse. It would surely take us a few days.

I bit my lower lip. My hands were sweaty. This was the biggest journey I ever went on. It was critical that I learned to control my magic. So much rested on my shoulders. What if I failed?
Steven squeezed my hand lovingly, whispering to me through our mate bond, "Everything will be fine, my love."
I was grateful to have such a loving mate. He was always there for me.

I looked around at everyone. Kate and Damien were in the royal chairs, embedded with golden threads. They were elevated above us. It made them look grand. Lilith and Zach were hunched over the map. They were pointing at different paths, talking lively about strategies. Blake, Elashor, and Arius were a little further near the corner of the table.

We were a strange bunch: an elf, two were-wolves, the daughter of the Moon Goddess, and four vampires.

We spoke about the journey, and the risks involved. It was agreed that once I mastered my powers, there was a possibility we would go fight Eurynomos directly. It was best to bring the strongest possible force to Mytvathyr, just in case. But we couldn't leave the castle defenseless either. There was also the question of Will. We didn't know if he'd join us along the way, or if he would succeed in defeating Eurynomos before us.

"Kate will stay at the castle. With her being pregnant, there's no way she's fighting a demon," stated, Damien.

Everybody nodded in agreement. This was evident to everyone. He continued, "I will stay here as well. With how things were when we arrived, I'm not letting her alone. I want to be there if the enemies breach the castle."

He turned to look at her, "I don't know what I would do if something were to happen to you or the baby."

I could feel Damien's love through his words. Kate had tears in her eyes. She was so moved.

"I want to stay here," stated Lilith. "I am the general. It's my duty to lead my troops into combat."

"Of course," agreed Damien.

"I'll stay as well," said Zach.

Lilith retorted, "You should go."

Zach looked at Lilith with wide eyes. "Are you sure?"

She smiled and kissed him on the cheek.

"You're strong, my love. I know you will survive. We can live all eternity together after the demon has been dealt with."

"Great!" exclaimed Steven. "Then I guess it's me, Bianca, and Zach."

Damien shook his head. "Blake is one of our best warriors. You've seen his worth against the orcs and goblins. He's coming with you as well."

"Don't forget us!" Arius grinned. "Elashor and I are strong too."

I was speechless. With the six of us, we would be a powerful force against the demon.

"Wow! Thank you, everyone," I spoke softly.

"You don't have to thank us," answered Steven. "We're doing this to get rid of this demon."

"And stop this war," added Zach.

"To be able to live in peace." Smiled Elashor.

"And so that Leila's sacrifice was not in vain," added Blake.

Everyone went silent. Everyone had their own reason to make this trip. I didn't know what awaited us, but I was happy to have my mate and my friends by my side.

Chapter 2 (Will)

Reunion

It didn't take me long to get to Montréal. I was flying low. I didn't care if people saw me or my dragon. They were attacked by the demon's army, anyway. There was no use trying to hide. Humans were aware of the existence of other races by now, anyway.

I kept flying towards downtown. I knew exactly where I needed to go. Damien had said enough when we were in the sacred grove of Ares. The entrance to the Underworld was in one of the subway stations. I didn't need more. I was sure to know which one it was. It was the biggest subway station in Montréal. It had multiple levels and connected all the other paths together.

I avoided a few skyscrapers as I got closer, maneuvering Ladon between them. I was glad to be riding such an agile dragon. The Grand Library of Montréal came into view. A magnificent tribute to culture and knowledge. Standing six floors tall, all covered in glass, and just beside it, the subway station I was looking for. The subway station looked small from the outside. That's because almost all of it was underground.

People were fighting against hordes of orcs and demons near the entrance. Bodies were piled up in the streets. Rivers of blood were flowing down the sewers. Rage filled my heart as I thought of all the lives that the demon had taken. Starting with the life of my mate. My heart sank and my wolf howled in agony at this thought. It was tearing me apart from the inside out, and I wondered if I could hold on through the pain. I brushed it away. Anger would be my fuel for what I needed to do.

Ladon lowered himself, getting ready to land on the ground. People looked up at the sky and saw us. They screamed and started running when they realized a dragon was nearby. If only they knew we were here to help them. There was no use in telling them. A gust of wind swept the ground as we landed, blowing dust and small debris around.

Orcs and demons started attacking us. I slashed through the enemies with the sword that had killed my beloved. Every time the sword would go through flesh, I would see the body of Leila in front of my eyes. With every kill, I was reminded of the tragedy that had happened only a few hours ago, tearing me up inside. Tears rolled down my cheeks as I grunted from the effort. I wanted to change into my wolf and decimate my enemies, but I couldn't. My wolf was hurting because of the loss of his mate. He shut himself off, and I was left alone to deal with my despair.

A demon charged at me. He had ram's horns, red glowing eyes and sharp teeth. His skin was white and wrinkled. His neck muscles were twice as large as his head. He was fighting with a double-edged war axe.
"You're mine!" he growled in a low, guttural voice.
He swung his axe at my sword. My legs trembled, threatening to give out from under me. My heart was racing, my lungs were hurting. I assembled whatever strength I had left, but he kept pushing on the axe, trying to make me give in.
Leila's lifeless body flashed in front of my eyes. Her sacrifice wouldn't be in vain. I let out a war cry as a second wind of energy filled my body.
"I won't let anyone stop me," I growled.

Rage and despair gave me a strength I didn't know I had. I pushed back the demon's axe and charged my shoulder into him, making him lose his balance. Swiftly, I swung my sword at him, blood was gushing out of his arm. He charged back with his axe, but I avoided his attack. We continued fighting for a while, but I eventually managed to sink my sword into his chest a few times.
The demon knelt panting, leaning on his war axe for support, a hand on his chest. Sweat and blood were dripping to the floor. He looked up at me as I lifted my sword in the air. In one big swing, I cut his head off. His body fell to the ground as his head rolled a few inches farther, blood pooling on the floor.

I looked around me and noticed Ladon had taken care of most of the enemies. A few human fighters had joined the fight as well. Eurynomos's army was dead. People were looking at me, afraid to come closer. I was covered in blood from head to toe. My clothes were dirty and torn. I couldn't care less about what people thought. I needed to get down to the subway station. But the subway station was way too small for Ladon to follow me into.

I concentrated on him. Although my wolf had shut himself off from me, he agreed to talk to Ladon for me, ordering him to get back to the vampire's castle. He would be safe with the others.

The dragon understood and immediately flew away southeast. I watched him for a moment before entering the subway station. The escalators were stopped. It smelled like foul urine. People had hidden from the demon's army here, making the subway station their refuge. They were lying on the floor and one corner of the station seemed to have become their bathroom. They turned their heads when I entered, but I paid them no attention. The only sounds were the whispers of people and the sound of my boots on the ground.

I made my way down the stairs, walked through the concrete tunnels, until I arrived at the first subway floor.

The trains had been stopped for a while, due to the demon's army attacks. More people were hiding here, crouched together. Mothers were trying to hush the cries of their children in fear of drawing attention. People were trying to hide themselves in the shadows of the walls as best they could. Their despair only made my anger towards Eurynomos grow. He was the cause of all our suffering. I wouldn't let him win.

An old man was standing. He was tall and thin. His clothes were ragged. His hair was long, white, and tangled. It looked like he hadn't shaved in days. He was missing a few teeth and smelled like he hadn't showered in weeks. He was laughing and shouting at everyone.
"The end is near! Prepare thyselves! The…"
He came to a sudden stop when he saw me.
He pointed his bony finger at me. "I've been waiting for you! What you seek is this way."
He pointed to the lower level of the tunnels on the far left.
"What do you mean, you've been waiting for me?"
I waited for an answer, but the old man only laughed and started chanting over, "It's the end. It's the end."
"You lost your mind, old fool," I whispered sourly.
He turned his head sharply, his gray eyes piercing me.
"I lost my mind, did I?"

He started running while laughing madly, jumping down the railing. Some people screamed and mothers hid their child's eyes with their hand. I ran to the railing to see the old man's corpse smashed against the floor below. People were circling him, looking at him horrified.

This man was surely mad, wasn't he? I thought about that as I made my way downstairs, to the lowest floor, towards the tunnel he had pointed at. This tunnel had been abandoned, and wooden panels blocked the way. I removed some of them to make myself a path. A strong smell of mold came out of the tunnel.

The tunnel was pitch-dark. Luckily, I had no problem seeing, thanks to my lycanthrope sight. Although I was beginning to worry about my wolf. I wasn't used to being cut off from him for such a long period of time. He had been with me for years, and now that he was silent, I felt strangely alone. Separated from my mate and from my wolf. I only hoped he would be able to recover and come back to me again.

Rats fled as I made my way into the old tunnel. The more I advanced, the less structured and maintained it was. The well-layered bricks started to make way to rocks and dirt. The tunnel started to look like it was dug right into the Earth's crust. A smell of sulfur now replaced the scent of mold. I kept going on and suddenly got to a strange opening.

It looked like a giant creature's head made of rock. Its eyes were round, and it looked like it was scared, or surprised. Its mouth was wide open, showing only two sharp canines at the top. A foul stench was coming out of its mouth. There was no other path than inside its mouth, where stairs seemed to lead the way down. There was no way I was going back, anyway. I carefully made my way into the strange opening, the scent of sulfur growing stronger.

I didn't need to prepare a lot of things for our upcoming trip. I got my sword sharpened and cleaned. Fighting with a blade had always been my favorite. It was mainly due to the fact that I was a human warrior before being turned into a vampire. Contrary to Arius and Damien, I wasn't born a vampire. I was dying on the battlefield when a woman took pity on me. She grabbed me and at first; I tried to resist. I was shocked by her force. She brought me with her. I was too weak to try to get away. When we got to her home, she laid me on a small bed in a dark room. I wondered what she wanted with me. Did she want to kill me? Then why save me on the battlefield? She opened her wrist and forced me to drink her blood. I remember the foul metallic taste of it. I was trying to turn my head away, not to drink it, but I couldn't. It was as if she was controlling my body, and maybe she was, now that I know better. After that, she left the room, leaving me alone on the bed. I didn't even have the time to think about running away, before every part of my body started to ache from the pain. I screamed in agony, contorting my body on the bed.

The woman came back, only stating these words, "Don't worry. You'll die soon enough."

I still remember the pain from my dying body. Death is so very cold. An icy feeling ran through my veins and the way my insides tore and ripped apart. The panic I felt when I realized I wasn't breathing anymore, but I was still alive… Then came a few days of tormenting sleep. I would have nightmares. I would dream of memories that weren't mine. Violent and bloody memories, waking up disoriented and dizzy. And the craving… A craving for blood, stronger than anything you could ever experience.

At first, Helena fed me. But she would only give a little blood at a time. She needed to be careful, or I could die during the transformation. I will never forget that intimate bond of feeding from her. I considered her to be my mother in death.

She was an amazing vampire. She taught me everything I know. How to feed, to keep my hunger in check. How to respect other races and how to behave myself. She also taught me to fine-tune my new vampiric senses and magic. I was happy with her.

Until the day some clerics found her and pierced her heart with a crucifix. I still remembered that day. The rage that filled me. I killed them all. Each one of them. Drank all of their blood. Nothing could ease my pain. I blindly fell into a rampage, killing every human that crossed my path. Until a young prince saw me. It was Damien. He was slightly older than me, but still young. He stopped me, brought me to the castle, to his father. Orpheus saw my potential and assigned me to train with the royal guards. Even though I had my vampire powers, I still preferred to fight with a sword. I guess it's the last reminder of my human life. I will be forever grateful to Damien. If it wasn't for him, I would surely have found death.

I got to the throne room. Everyone was already there. I bowed my head to Damien. He nodded back.

Arius stated, "Roads are impracticable because of the demon's army."

Bianca asked, "Should we take the dragons, then?"

Damien shook his head. "The dragons should stay here to help with the castle's defense."

"Then how are we going to travel?" asked Bianca.

"We should take horses, and travel through the forest," answered, Steven.

Flying wasn't an option. Elashor was elven, Bianca was human, and Steven was a wolf. Horses weren't my favorite, but it was the next best thing, and it would get us to our destination.

Kate announced, "I had tents and food prepared for your journey. You will need to rest somewhere along the way, as it will take you at least a full day to get there."

"We'd better get going, then," I replied.

Everyone nodded. Goodbyes were said.

Damien came to see me. "I know you'll make me proud, my friend."

I smiled at him.

"Thank you, my lord. I will do my best."

We began our journey, traveling north-east, towards Mytvathyr. We brought no extra baggage. Everyone had their horse. The tents and supplies had been distributed all over the horses. We traveled in silence. Even the birds were silent. I usually enjoy riding, but today, my arms were tense, my hands were griping the reins. From afar, we could hear the sound of the demon's army fighting. Luckily, they wouldn't hear the hooves of the horses on the grass. It's not that we couldn't fight them, but we needed to get to Mytvathyr as fast as possible. If we wanted to stop those battles, we needed Bianca to control her powers, swiftly.

We traveled for a while, always hiding in the forest. The horses had no trouble avoiding the branches of the trees, but the ground was somewhat uneven, forcing us to slow down. The last thing we'd want would be for a horse to hurt its hoof on a rock. After a few hours, we came to a small clearing in the forest. Dead leaves covered the ground. The sun was already setting as it set early at this time of year. To the east, we could see a mountain top appearing over the trees. We were now far enough from the main roads that we didn't hear the demon's army anymore.

"This sounds like a great place to camp," suggested Arius.

"I agree," I answered. "We should be deep enough in the woods that we won't be attacked."

We tied the horses to trees and gave them food and water. Zach and Arius went to scout the area and gather firewood, while Steven started a fire. It was cold, and we needed the fire's heat to warm us. I helped Bianca and Elashor set up the tents and get some food ready. We had brought basic supplies. It wouldn't be a feast, but it would be good enough.

*********** Kate's POV ***********

I sat on my bed, exhausted from the battle against the demon's army and from being pregnant. It was taking a toll on my body. But at least Damien was back. I had been so afraid he wouldn't come back! I knew he was the Vampire Lord, but I was afraid he would be killed. I would have been crushed if something had happened to my mate.

"Are you alright?" Damien asked in a soft voice as he sat on the bed beside me.

I nodded to him.

"Yes, I just feel tired, that's all."

I rested my head on his shoulder. My heart fluttered as his manly scent surrounded me. My wolf screamed, "Mate!" in my head, wagging her tail. She didn't like to be separated from him, even just for a few days. I hadn't realized how much I missed him. He put his hand on my stomach. His touch was cool and refreshing. My belly was still flat, yet I could feel a warm little bundle of love growing inside it.

"I want to help you as best I can. Let me handle all the stress from the war. You just concentrate on yourself and the baby."

"I missed you so much," I whispered.

He cupped my cheek with his hand.

"I know. I'm sorry I've been away."

I looked at him with wide eyes. How could he say such a thing? "You were away to break my sister's curse. You have nothing to apologize for!"

His hair was tied in a low bun, his gray eyes filled with sadness.

"Yet, I don't know what I would have done if something were to have happened to you or the baby…"

I got closer to him, my lips brushing against his.

"But it didn't. I'm here."

He looked at me, as if noticing me for the first time, and smirked.

"How lucky I am."

His lips crushed on mine with a sudden need. I played with his hair, getting them loose as we kissed. He tasted so good. My wolf was over-joyed to have her mate to herself again. He gently pushed me to the bed and got on top of me, making sure not to put his weight on my stomach.

"I missed you," he purred, his words rolling on my skin.

A deep rumble reverberated through his chest.

"I love when you do that," I whispered.

He smirked. "Then I'll make sure to do it more often."

He left a trail of kisses on my skin, making goosebumps rise everywhere he touched. I gasped when he licked the mark on my neck. The mark he made when he mated me years ago. He lingered there for a moment. Heat spread at my core when I felt the tip of his fangs grazing at the spot.

"Damien," I whimpered, "do it."

He inhaled deeply and nibbled my earlobe.

"Not yet, my little wolf."

He removed my shirt, his fingers roaming over my skin.

"Always so gorgeous!" he exclaimed in a husky voice.

His eyes were filled with hunger and desire. I removed his shirt while he removed my bra. How I missed seeing his muscled chest. I loved to roam his chest with my hands, feeling the hard muscles. I gasped as he licked my nipples, getting them hard. I grabbed his pants, getting them undone, as he kept licking my breasts. His hard cock sprang in front of me when I finally got his pants off.

"I'm not done with you yet, my little wolf." He smirked as he removed my pants and panties. I gasped as he brushed his finger at my opening.

He smirked. "Already so wet for me."

I grabbed the sheets and moaned as he inserted a finger into my opening. Fuck, I hadn't realized how much I needed him! I cursed when he started to rub my clit, making me arch my back as pleasure started to build up.

"Damien," I whined.

He smiled as he watched me writhe from his touch. I moaned loudly as he kept rubbing, knowing exactly how to pleasure me.

"Won't you cum for me, little wolf?"

He didn't need to ask, as I was already on the verge. His eyes flashed with hunger as I came hard, my walls pulsing around his fingers.

"Good girl."

He came back up, kissing me with passion. The tip of his cock was pushing at my entrance, making me yearn for more.

He whispered in a husky voice, "I love you so much, my little wolf."

I gasped as his hard cock filled me completely. This moment was perfect, with him inside of me, surrounded by his scent, and feeling truly loved. He thrust inside of me, adjusting himself to my cries. I grabbed onto his shoulders. I could feel his pleasure from our mate bond, bringing me even further, as I felt myself tighten around his cock.

He started to lick my neck as he kept thrusting inside of me, my nipples brushing against his chest. My heart was racing. I cried in pleasure when he bit me on the neck. He groaned as he drank my blood and thrust harder. Never in my life did I feel more complete than in this moment. I could feel his love and passion through our mate bond. Our hearts beating together in unison as I was connected to him more than ever.

"Oh yes! Damien!" I screamed as I climaxed again, my walls pulsing around him.

He thrust hard a little more, sending wave after wave of pleasure, until he grunted hard as he came. He removed his teeth from my neck, and lingered there for a moment, closing the wound.

"Hm… I love when you scream my name, my little wolf," he whispered into my ear, his lips brushing on my earlobe.

I turned my head a little so I could look at him. His lips were on mine before I could even say anything, his tongue dancing with mine. A soft purr was rumbling through his chest, causing my wolf to purr in response.

"I will always love you with all that I am," he added, his haunting gray eyes staring into my soul. I whispered back, "So will I, my mate."

We laid together for a while, basking in each other's love. I truly hoped that this was what paradise felt like. Damien still had his hand on my stomach. Ever since I discovered I was expecting, he had been doing this. I thought it was so sweet. I felt grateful to have such a caring mate.

"Your blood tastes different."

I looked at him with questioning eyes. "Really?"

"Yes. It changed because of the baby. I can't say yet if it's a girl or a boy, but I can feel the baby growing inside of you; in your blood."

I smiled at his comment. It must be nice to be able to feel the baby this way. I was feeling all the changes in my body. And I knew that in a few months I would feel it moving inside of me in a way only I could be able to feel. But I felt happy that he could feel it this way, too.

"I can already say our baby will be strong and wonderful."

His voice was full of love for our baby to come. I asked worryingly, "Will there be a kingdom for our child to grow in?"

The war with the demon was scaring me. What will the world be like when he's born? Damien cupped my face with his hand, staring into my soul.

"Don't you worry, my little wolf. We'll make sure there is a world for our baby to grow up in." His words were so full of confidence; I knew he would do whatever it took to make it happen.

A loud noise outside, followed by the roar of a dragon got us out of bed. Damien put his pants on in a hurry. I grabbed my bathrobe and went to the balcony. A massive dragon stood beside Cara. He had six heads. His scales were black with blueish-turquoise reflections. Each of its scales glittered with a unique fire. He looked powerful. He was truly magnificent!

"Is that…?"

Damien answered, "Ladon."

I looked around, but Will was nowhere to be seen.

I asked anxiously, "Then where is Will?"

Damien put his arm around my shoulders. "I have no idea."

Cara rubbed her head affectionately on Ladon as he laid in the castle's yard to rest. She cuddled with him, laying by his side. He wrapped his tail around her. It was beautiful to see their love expressed this way.

But as beautiful as it was, I was worried about Will. I thought he would have come back with his dragon. This meant he was either dead, or still out there fighting against Eurynomos. He lost his mate. I didn't know what I'd do if I lost Damien, but I've heard of many stories of werewolves going crazy after losing their mates. I only hoped he was fine.

I remember how Will was always so serious. His duties always came first. The pack was so important to him. Would he come back to take care of his pack?

I remember when we played together, him, Bianca, Steven, and I. We were always so close. We used to play in the woods for hours. There was this river flowing nearby. The terrain was steep, and Will had warned us not to venture there. But Bianca, Steven, and I were reckless and loved to contradict Will. Bianca had slipped on the rocks and twisted her ankle. I had run back to get Will. He had been so worried when I told him about Bianca. He had run to her and carried her in his arms all the way to the pack's house. He had taken the blame for what had happened, so she didn't get grounded by our parents. He had cared for her, kept her company, until she was completely nursed back to health. He was always so eager to protect the people he loved. I only wished I could protect him now. Was he even still alive?

I tried not to think about that possibility. I didn't want to believe he was dead. I buried my nose in the crook of Damien's neck, deeply inhaling his musk and honey scent that I loved so much. He hugged me tightly.

I looked across the courtyard to see Elwin and Ravynne, sitting on a bench. They were talking together, smiling. It looked like they were getting to know each other. It was the first time I saw the old sorcerer smile like that. I felt happy that he had found someone to open up to. Ravynne seemed quite happy too, though I hadn't known her for a long time. It was a sweet reminder that friendship found its way at all ages and across all races.

Chapter 3 (Bianca)

Mytvathyr

We sat by the fire. Elashor was signing a song in her elvish language. It was so beautiful to hear her sing. Arius watched her lovingly as she sang.

"Hôwm jë lông thô ëtry buÿ yôr sidë, muÿ lôvigne knittë.[1] Will yôou lëtt më fill yôr nitts avëc

---

[1] *How I long to be by your side, my loving knight. Will you let me fill your nights with passion? Let me kiss those lips of yours, for my heart beats for you.*

passiô? Lëtt më kiss tôsë lèvrës ôhv yôrs, fôr muÿ härt beëts fôr yôou."

Zach and Blake talked together while eating.

I rested my head on Steven's shoulder. It feels like it's been ages since I've spent an evening alone with him. We had been so busy with the war preparations. Tonight, I wanted to believe we were alone. The problems and worries could wait until tomorrow.

"Tonight, you're mine," Steven spoke through our mate bond. I knew it came from his wolf; I could feel the need in his words. It was raw and possessive. It came from deep within him and made me yearn with desire. I wanted to be his.

I whispered in his ear, "I'll always be yours, my mate."

He smirked and kissed me. A deep rumble came from his chest. I knew his wolf was happy. I lost track of time as Steven caressed my back, whispering sweet nothings in my ear, the warmth of his body surrounding me. I surrendered myself to his kisses, leaving out everything else.

Steven's wolf growled, "Mine."

I giggled softly.

"Sorry," said Steven, embarrassed. "It's getting harder and harder to keep him in check."

I smiled at him. I knew how much he wanted to mark me, to make me his forever.

"Soon, my love. Like I told you, you can mark me after we've dealt with the demon."

He nodded.

"Do you even know how hard it is? My wolf is constantly begging me to do it. To sink my teeth into that sweet neck of yours."

"I know. But you know that I'll fall into heat if you do. I can't have anything distracting me until we kill this demon."

"Yes, I know."

He looked defeated. I cupped his chin and stared into his blue eyes.

"You are my mate. I will never stop loving you. Soon, my love. I promise."

He smiled and kissed me once more.

I looked around us, to realize everyone had gone to bed already.

"Maybe we should get to sleep, too. We have a long day ahead of us tomorrow."

Steven chuckled lowly.

"Yes, you're right."

The fire was already out, anyway. We went into our tent. I hadn't even realized how tired I was.

We laid down together. Steven held me tight as I fell to slumber.

I woke up wrapped up in Steven's arms, surrounded by his scent. He was looking at me, a smile on his face.

"Hey there, sleeping beauty."

I smiled at his remark.

"Hi," I simply answered before kissing him.

He kissed me back, his tongue making its way into my mouth. He roamed my body with his hands, making his way between my legs.

"Steven!" I whispered as he started to rub my clit.

He smirked. "They won't hear us."

Pleasure started to build up inside of me. I tried to get my hands on his bulge, wanting to please him too, but he was out of reach, as he was taller than me.

"I can't reach you," I whimpered between moans.

"I know," he said with a wink. "Now, won't you cum for me?"

His eyes were full of desire. He was in control, and all I could do was squirm from his touch.

He kissed me to muffle my moans. A few seconds later, I bucked my back as I came, waves of pleasure washing over me.

Steven smirked. "Gorgeous!"

My pulse was racing when he aligned himself with me and penetrated my still pulsing core. A feeling of ecstasy took me over and I dug my fingers into his shoulders.

"Fuck," he groaned as we made love.

He adjusted his thrusts to my cries, bringing me to the brink again. I could feel his wolf wanting to come out, to mark me, but Steven only grazed at my neck with his fangs. It didn't take long for me to cum again. He came almost at the same time from the moment I climaxed.

"I love you so much," Steven whispered in my ear. "You're the best thing that ever happened to me. If forever exists, let it be with you."

My heart fluttered at his words.

"Aww Steven, I'm sure it does. We'll get to spend it together."

He showered me with kisses again.

We heard some noise outside our tent. The others were already up. I giggled.

"Perhaps we should get dressed and join them."

Steven grinned. "Do we really have to?"

I winked. "You know we do."

We quickly got up and exited the tent. Breakfast was served. Arius was talking with Elashor.

"Bônn mômigne.[2]"

Elashor smiled at him.

"Bônn,"[3] she answered. "You're improving at it. But you still need to get better."

He smirked and winked.

"That's funny. That's not what you were saying last night."

Elashor's cheeks turned red as she put a hand on her mouth, looking frantically to see if anyone had heard his comment. I refrained myself from giggling and pretended I hadn't heard.

"Don't say that! What if people hear you?"

He laughed and teased her.

"What *if* people heard me? What would they think?"

---

[2] Good morning.

[3] Good

She blathered, not knowing what to answer. He grabbed her in his arms, kissing and tickling her.

I sat and started to eat breakfast with Steven. Zach and Blake were with us as well.

"Think we'll reach the town today?" I asked Zach.

He nodded.

"We're probably not that far."

Thinking about this made me think about Will. I felt so bad that his mate died because of me. A knot formed in my stomach. I wasn't so hungry all the sudden.

"Are you okay?" asked Blake.

I shook my head, a lone tear rolling down my cheek.

"I'm feeling so bad about Will. He lost his mate because of me. And now, he's trying to fight a demon all by himself. I'm so scared he's going to get killed!"

I couldn't hold this torrent that was pouring. This feeling of guilt was eating me. If it weren't because of me, Will would still be with Leila. Steven gently cuddled me into his arm, kissing me on the neck.

"First," started Blake, "I was there. Leila chose to be sacrificed. She wanted to face her destiny. It had nothing to do with you."

"It had everything to do with me and my stupid curse!" I exclaimed between sobs.

"No, it didn't," continued Blake. "Ravynne told us. Every generation, someone from their pack was born under a blessed night, born with a special marking. These people were destined to be sacrificed to keep the demon at bay."

"But they didn't do that anymore," I replied. "That's how they became a rogue pack in the first place."

Blake didn't agree with me. "Maybe, but it was still her destiny. She chose to fight, and so we should fight to honor her sacrifice."

I stopped crying and thought about what he just said. He was right. She chose to fight. We needed to keep fighting, too. And that's exactly what we were doing by going to the elven city. I nodded slowly.

"Still, it doesn't make me feel better about it."

Steven gently caressed my cheek.

"I know, my love. But it will be fine. You're not alone. Don't forget who you are. You're the Moon Goddess's daughter!"

I stayed in his arms, resting my head on his chest while I finished eating breakfast. They were right; I knew it. I hoped I could stop feeling guilty about what had happened. I knew I had it in me. I knew I could be strong. I sucked in a breath, determined to shove this guilt aside and concentrate on the task at hand. I needed to learn to master my new powers.

We packed our things in no time and were back on the horses. We traveled in the woods again. The trees looked lifeless with their leaves on the ground. A cold breeze was blowing, reminding us that winter would come soon enough. You could see the breath vapor from the horses in the cold air. I felt lucky that I had my coat to keep me warm.

After a few hours, we started to see Mytvathyr from afar. I couldn't believe how pretty it was! The city was so big! It was surrounded by waterfalls and very tall trees. These trees were probably hundreds of years old. Several of them were taller than the buildings. Some houses looked like they were carved into the trees themselves. Tall rocky walls surrounded the city, and I could only see a part of the city. I couldn't wait to get there and see it up close.

We arrived at the city a few hours later. The gates were closed. Two elven guards stood at the gates. They looked at us sternly.

"Halt! You shall not pass."

I was baffled and answered, "I don't understand. I've been told this city was friendly."

"Due to recent attacks, the city has been closed by the King and the Queen. Only elves may enter."

I frowned at them.

The guards pointed to Elashor. "Only she can enter."

Elashor shook her head. "There's no way I'm going to the city without my friends."

Then she added, "Häs failôwm ëlvz, wônte yôou ëlpe anotre[4] ûnn?"

The guards frowned.

"Daïsôlé. Kïnggz ôrdres.[5]"

Elashor pouted her lips.

---

[4] As fellow elves, won't you help another one?

[5] Sorry. King's order.

I asked the guards, "Can we talk with the King and the Queen? We were sent here by the vampire Lord and his queen."

The two guards looked surprised by my statement. They stared at each other, not knowing what to answer. They studied us carefully. The first guard answered, "Follow us."

While the first guard opened the gates of the city, the second one added, "Try anything funny, and I'll cut you down." He looked so dead serious; I didn't dare answer anything.

We followed them into the city. It was even more beautiful inside the walls. We walked on the cobblestone path towards the palace. Elven architecture was so elegant, blending itself with nature. They combined stones and woods with glass to create marvels of architecture. We passed dozens of houses and shops of all kinds. Whether you needed clothes, food, weapons, or armor, this city seemed to have it all. There was even a bookshop, and I wondered if there were a lot of elven authors.

People went about their business, glancing at us as we passed. They were all elven. There were the dark elves, with their black ebony skin. Their eyes glowed, ranging from ice blue to dark red. A few of them had gray skin and white hair. I guessed they were the gray elves. A lot of them were high elves. They were easily recognizable by their yellowish skin. They were renowned to be the best at magic but liked to stay amongst themselves. They didn't like to meddle in others' problems. We even crossed paths with a few moon elves, snow elves, wood elves, and a winged elf. I had no idea what race that one was. I had never heard of a winged elf. She was breathtaking!

A kid pointed to us, whispering to his mother, "Mômm. Lôukë.[6]"

She scolded him, "Dôntë pôïngt ätt peëapl[7]."

I wasn't sure what this was about, but I couldn't help but to think it was funny how mothers had to scold their kids the same way, whatever the race or language.

A little further, we arrived at the palace. It stood in the center of the city. It was a wonder to look at. Its towers danced with the clouds. The sun reflected on the various windows, painting a colorful array on the cobblestone path below. Paths seemed to float between the various towers of the castle. There were even a few observatory stations where people could look at the view or meditate peacefully.

---

[6] Mom. Look.

[7] Don't point at people.

I wished I could have admired it longer, but the guards took us directly to the throne room. People whispered things as we passed by. We were the only human, werewolves, and vampires around. I guessed they didn't see our kinds often. Even Elashor was staying close to Arius, holding his hand tightly. I was happy to have Steven by my side. Knowing he was there with me and feeling the warmth of his body nearby was enough to make me feel better.

Servants brought plates and platters full of food that smelled divine. They were glancing at us while we passed. One of them was a dark elf. Her hair was purplish red on top, with the tips being fiery red. Her yellowish glowing gaze seemed to hold untold secrets. Seeing she was observed, she quickly returned her eyes to the floor, resuming her servants' duties.

The King was sitting on his throne. He was tall and had a pale yellowish skin. His hair was blond, going down his shoulders. His eyes were yellow and green. His eyelids were so dark, it looked like he had makeup, making his eye color pop out even more. His brows were dark and severe. He had a manly yet graceful look. His crown was made of obsidian intersected with golden leaves.

The Queen was sitting by his side. She had long blond hair with braids on each side of her head. Her skin was almost white, and her eyes were deep blue. Her red lips contrasted with her skin color, like a rosebud in snow. Her crown was made of delicate gold threads braided together, with an aquamarine jewel going down her forehead. Her beauty was that of a delicate flower bestowing its fragrance upon us in the gentle summer breeze.

The guards bowed before them. We did the same.

"Your Majesty! Those outsiders asked for an audience with you," one of the guards stated, keeping his head down.

"Who might you be?" asked the King.

I raised my eyes, unsure of how to proceed in front of the King.

"I am Bianca, daughter of the Moon Goddess. We were sent here by the vampire Lord and his queen. We seek your aid."

The King raised a brow at my statement.

"And what could the mighty vampire Lord and the Moon Goddess's daughter possibly need of us?"

I wasn't sure where I should start. I got the feeling it was better to keep it short.

"We need to consult with the magic guild. I need to learn to control my magic. If I can have any chances at fighting the demon, Eurynomos, who is bestowing war on us."

The King took a moment to think. His face was stern and didn't filter any of his emotions. My heart was racing. So much depended on me being able to control my magic powers.

"I'm afraid it's not possible."

His words crushed my hopes. I knew I needed to keep my composure in front of the King, but I wanted to protest. It was so important that I learned to use my magic.

He continued, "Recently, harpies, centaurs, goblins, orcs, and even demons, have been attacking the city. Many people died. The magic guild members are assigned to the city's protection and to healing our people."

My mind was racing, trying to find something to answer, anything!

"Please, your Majesty!" started Blake, but the King made a movement with his arm, asking him to be silent.

"You must leave," started the Queen. "The city is now a sanctuary for our kind. We can't even venture into the woods anymore without fearing an attack. We can't afford to have outsiders in the city. I hope you can understand."

Her voice was kind and full of care for her people. They were only trying to protect themselves against the demon's army. They didn't understand that we were there to stop the demon. It was the only way the attacks would ever stop.

I wanted to reply something, when a guard barged into the room.

"King Alluin, Queen Solandra, we are under attack! Some kids are trapped in a grove nearby, encircled by the enemies. Succubi are approaching the gates. We need to defend the city!"

The King stood from his throne.

"This is your fault!" he pointed at us. "I'm sure the demon's army followed you here. We never had succubus attacks before."

We all looked at each other and nodded.

"Let's take care of them," Zach said out loud what we were all thinking.

We left the throne room in a hurry, not waiting for the guards, running towards the city's entrance. There was no way we'd let the demon's army destroy this city or kill innocent children.

*********** Will's POV ***********

The air felt hotter as I got lower. Luckily, all my years of training had prepared my body to endure such a harsh environment. But I was hurting so much from the mate bond severing. I felt like my body could crumble to pieces. My wolf was wounded and silent. I only hoped I would be strong enough to avoid my wolf taking over and falling into bloodlust. That's why I needed to hurry. I had to slit the throat of the one responsible for my mate's death before I lost what little control I had. In my mind, I kept seeing Leila's lifeless body. My arms still felt like they held her body. I should have found a way to save her. I was the worst mate ever, letting her sacrifice herself like that. I would be forever guilty of her death. Anger filled me as I realized how much I had failed her.

I soon came to a big opening. It was dark; the air was foul. The scent of ashes filled the air, and it was incredibly hot. I rejoiced to myself. Surely, this was the underworld. This world was like a dismal nightmare, a world inhabited by shadows, barren of hope, ill-lit and desolated.
My lungs hurt from the soaring heat and my eyes burned from the sulfur, but I was stronger than that. I made my way towards the Styx, the muddy black river. I knew I had to cross its poisonous waters to get to Eurynomos. I went to the shore, staring into the river of hatred and unbreakable oaths. I swore I would avenge Leila's death.

I saw a ferry approach the shore where dozens of souls were waiting to board, their gold coin in hand. I knew the ferryman was Charon, an emaciated old skeleton. I didn't have a gold coin, but surely, I could find a way to reason with him. I smirked.

I let the souls board the ferry. Charron held out his long bony fingers for me to place a coin in his hand as I tried to board the ferry.

I gritted through my teeth, "I don't have a coin."

He stared harshly at me with his hollow eyes. He was the one making the rules here and didn't like me trying to defy them. But I wasn't about to let anyone stop me.

"No coin, no passage."

His tone was threatening. People got further back in the ferry, trying to get away from us. I taunted him further, making my intentions clear. I got one step closer as I replied harshly.

"I'm not here to play. You will bring me to the other side."

Green flames lit in Charron's empty eye sockets. A magic wind passed through my body as he motioned with his arm.

"No one breaks the rules."

He was furious. I could feel he was holding back his power. It was only a warning, and I was wondering why he didn't attack me fully. Was his power so great that he needed to hold back? I pushed that thought aside. It didn't matter; I had every reason to fight. I swung the sacred sword at his arm, dislodging the arm from his shoulder.

Charron grunted. He ignored me and picked up his arm, reattaching it to his body.

"Are you so eager to die? You foolish mortal!"

He sent a bolt of magic to my knee. The pain spread from my leg to my body, getting me to the ground, paralyzing my body. I panted as I waited for my body to move again.

"I'm not the one… who's going to die."

I spoke with effort as I fought to get back up, my body shaking from the effort, beads of sweat pooling on my skin.

"You pathetic creature!" spat Charron. "Can't you see how weak you are? Brought to your knees with just a fraction of my powers. Why are you so eager to die?"

I cursed. He was more powerful than I thought. If he was so powerful, then how strong was Eurynomos?

I roared with anger, "I have things to deal with, with Eurynomos, and you will not keep me from it."

Charron suddenly smirked, his face lighting up with an evil force I didn't think was possible.

"Oh! So, you wish to speak with the master, then why didn't you say so?"

His smile was vile and twisted.

"I guess I can make an exception, then," he added, while letting me board his boat.

Stunned, I waited a few seconds. Was it a trap? Why did he change his mind so suddenly? I walked on board the boat.

"You better rest while we cross. You're going to need it."

I didn't like his tone. He gave up too easily. Did he want me to confront Eurynomos? Was there a trap waiting for me on the other side? He was so powerful; he could have crushed me like a bug. It didn't fit, but at least I got a free ride on the ferry.

The boat glided silently across the dark waters of the Styx. My body felt better, and my strength was renewed. I kept glancing at Charron. I didn't trust that old skeleton at all. Everything in me was telling me to be vigilant. I expected to be attacked at any moment. Dark thoughts clouded my mind. Was I crazy to try to fight Eurynomos? Would I ever stand a chance? I couldn't even fight Charron on the ferry. How could I hope to defeat Eurynomos ? No matter, I would avenge Leila's death, or die trying.

As we approached the other side of the Styx, I could see countless portals spawned. The demon's army was waiting to cross to the world of the livings. Although some of them were more composed, like the succubi, some others were mindless stupid creatures, fighting with each other, like the orcs. I would surely have to fight my way through them to get to Eurynomos.

A large structure stood at the center of Tartarus. This must surely be where he resided. I couldn't wait to get there and kill the bastard. Nothing would prevent me from killing Leila's murderer. Vengeful energy burned through my veins, making my heart beat with anger, keeping my body going. I gripped my sword as the boat finally docked to the other shore, bracing myself for the fight to come.

Chapter 4 (Blake)

A Black Diamond

We were back at the city gates in no time. It was easy to follow the sound of battle. Succubi were teaming up with the harpies, attacking from the air. Orcs and centaurs were attacking on the ground, fighting with the elven guards. It was evident they were getting overwhelmed. We could hear screams from children a little further up.

"I'll help the kids. You guys take care of the ones here," shouted Zach to us, before shifting to his wolf form, his favorite levitating sword following him. He kept impressing me with his speed and strength. Surely, he wouldn't have trouble dealing with whatever was at the grove attacking the children.

Steven shifted as well, preferring to fight in his wolf form. Bianca threw balls of elemental magic at the succubi and harpies, getting them to the ground. From there, Steven and Elashor would attack them. While Steven decimated them with his claws and teeth, Elashor would slash through them with her dual swords. Arius and I tackled the orcs and centaurs.

Arius was a powerful vampire Prince. He loved to use his vampire's powers on his enemies, killing them with magic, or drinking their blood. But for me, nothing will ever replace the feeling of my sword piercing the enemies. It was making the blood rush through my veins, adrenaline pumping through my body.

My eyes flashed at the scent of blood, reminding me it's been a few days since I've properly fed. Maybe I should make an exception today, I thought as I jumped on a centaur, sinking my teeth in his neck, drinking his life away. He tried to struggle, but I used my vampiric powers to hold him down. The blood began to leave his body, as did his will to fight. I drank every last drop. As the blood entered my system, I felt every fiber of my body restore itself. It was a euphoric feeling, and I never got tired of it.

Once I was properly restored, I slashed through the remaining enemies until there were none left standing.

The elven guards looked exhausted, but there were only a few casualties.

"Let's see if Zach and the children are okay," shouted, Bianca.

We ran to the grove to see piles of dead goblins lying on the ground. Zach was still in his wolf form. The kids were hiding behind bushes.

They spoke timidly, "Prôszę, dôntë eëtte ôssë.[8]"

I had no idea what they were saying. Elashor smiled and advanced towards them gently.

She told them softly, "Dôntë ëtry scarëde. Wiï wônte härmm yôou.[9]"

She knelt by Zach's wolf and started to pet him gently. He seemed to get where she was going and laid down on the ground, resting his head on his front paws. The kids peeked from behind the bushes. A little girl timidly came forward and started to pet the wolf. Seeing there was no danger,

---

[8] Please, don't eat us.

[9] Don't be scared. We won't harm you.

the other kids came out of hiding, too. The incentive of petting a wolf seemed to overpower the fear of what had happened earlier.

I stayed away, not wanting to scare them. After a while, some of them were even laughing. I refrained from laughing, thinking how this powerful vampire-werewolf was playing nice with the children.

"Cômm, lëtts gëtte yôou hômm[10]," Elashor said, as she stood up, offering her hand to the children.

The little girl grabbed her hand. The other kids followed as we walked together back to the city. As we approached the city's walls, some elven adults came running, hugging their kids.

The guards from earlier approached us.

"Come, let us report to the King."

We followed them back to the castle. As we entered the throne room, a young servant passed in front of us, bringing the meals to the King and Queen. A growl reverberated through my chest as it did earlier when I first noticed her. Never in my life had a woman had any effect on me. But somehow, she stirred emotions inside of me I barely comprehended.

---

[10] Come, let's get you home.

Truly, she was magnificent. A black diamond hiding in plain sight, waiting to be picked. Her hair was purplish on top, then red as fire. Her eyes were yellow and her lips were bright red. A yellow flower was glowing, embedded in her skin, resting on her chest just above her breasts, as a permanent jewel. I had never seen anything like it. My body was pulled to her. All I could think of was how I'd love to sink my fangs into her skin and claim her. If that's what it felt like to find your mate, I could understand why their bond lasted forever.

She raised her eyes for a moment, staring at my soul. I was almost sure she could feel it, too. I could smell her scent all the way from where I was. An irresistible scent of peaches and spices that was intoxicating me. I wondered if she tasted as good as she smelled. She lowered her eyes and got the plates on the royal table.

I got pulled out of my thoughts by the King.

"The guards already relayed what happened. You have done this city a great service. We have decided to let you stay in the city."

This was great news. We really needed Bianca to master her powers as fast as possible. This demon needed to be dealt with.

"You are free to visit the city, and the magic guild. Rooms will be made available for you when you come back," added the Queen.

I bowed my head in front of the King and Queen.

"Thank you, Your Majesty!" said Arius.

"Eshenesra!" yelled a man from the kitchen. "Come here, you incompetent wench. You would know to do your tasks with care if you don't want to end up doing the stable chore again."

The woman jumped at the sound of that man's voice. So, Eshenesra was her name, I pondered. What a beautiful name.

I couldn't appreciate it, though, not the way that man was talking to her. I gritted my teeth, reminding myself I was in front of the King and Queen; who did nothing to intervene.

A little fat elf rushed into the room, looking angrily at Eshenesra. Passing by her side, he bumped into her, making her drop a bowl of soup on the floor.

He started to yell insults at her as she wiped the soup from the floor with her apron. Her clothes were stained, her lips were trembling, tears flowed on her cheeks silently.

I watched the scene clenching my fists. Anger boiled inside of me. I wanted to help her so badly, but couldn't do anything. I didn't want to cause any political problems. We just had been granted the right to stay in the city and in the castle.

But the truth is, I wanted to rip that man's head off. The way he talked to my Eshenesra was unacceptable. Did I just say, "My"? I guess I did… The only way I could explain how I felt for her was that she was my fated mate. And as her mate, it was also my duty to protect her. And it killed me inside to watch helplessly as this man yelled at her.

"Let's get to the city." Zach's hand came to rest on my shoulder, making me turn my head, and stop looking at my mate. I nodded to him, then looked back to my beautiful mate, still on the floor.

Eshenesra's sad eyes landed on me. In this moment, I wanted to take her in my arms, to shelter her, to wipe her tears, and protect her. I wished I could tell her so many things right now.

Reluctantly, I turned around and followed everyone outside the castle, into the city.

*********** Eshenesra's POV ***********

Once again reprimanded for something I didn't do. How I hated Scalanis! He's been mistreating me for years. Ever since I turned down his advances, he's made it his duty to piss me off as much as he could. My clothes were stained. The burning soup traveled through my clothes, to my skin, where it burned for a while before cooling. I felt so ashamed he scolded me in front of those strangers. Especially in front of that tall warrior who was watching me. I could feel the weight of his stare on my shoulders. He looked very strong. I loved how his black hair came to his shoulders. I couldn't help noticing the tattoos completely covering one of his arms.

But I was a fool for even having these thoughts. No one could love someone like me; a poor servant at the castle. Being born a dark elf, I was condemned to a life of servitude from the very beginning.

I was born without magic, and I couldn't wield an arc. My parents were cruelly killed in front of me when I was just a child, in the great revolt against our kind. I was spared, since I was only a child, but I often wished they had decided to kill me too. At least I wouldn't have to endure all of this.

Now, I was stuck serving high elves. Their race had hated us for generations, not even trying to hide their disdain for us. Although the King and the Queen had always been kind to me, Scalanis was a vile elf. He hated me and didn't try to hide it. He was the chief of the servant's quarters. The King has always ignored the way Scalanis spoke to me.

Scalanis knew how to hit me so that it didn't leave a mark. Or that no one could see the mark. Surely, the King and the Queen wouldn't tolerate someone hitting me. Or maybe they would? I wasn't sure anymore. Nobody would believe me anyway. My voice was against the voice of the servant's chief. Everyone feared him. He made sure of that. And if any of us tried to stand up to him, he would make an example out of it. No one would dare to contradict him.

I quickly picked up everything that was on the floor. I knew that if I weren't fast enough, he would correct me when no one would see.

One day, I hoped to live freely in the city. I knew that many dark elves lived freely in the city. I went to see them on the rare occasions when I had a day off. Or I would simply meet them in the streets, on my way to get supplies for the castle.

This city was supposed to be a shelter for all elven races, living in harmony together.

"Eshenesra!" yelled Scalanis from the servants' quarters. I gritted my teeth at the vile elf's voice. One day I would tell him all my hatred. One day, I would stand up to him and make him pay. But for now, I needed to obey.

"Coming," I answered before getting there in a hurry.

Damien had left a few hours ago to check on the training of fighters and recruits. In recent days, there had been an increase in the number of people wanting to fight with us. A lot of them had little to no fighting experience. It was imperative to train them, and fast. Especially since with the current pace of attacks, they may need to go into battle sooner rather than later. To send them into combat without training would be to send them to a certain death.

I checked the improvised infirmary in the ballroom. I was pleasantly surprised to see that Elwin and Ravynne had managed to get all the wounded back to health. They might not all be fully ready to head back into battle, but it was better than what I expected.

I made my way towards the courtyard to check on the repairs. The main gate had been repaired. Fortifications were being built. Ravynne was standing at the center of the courtyard. Her eyes were closed, her hands clasped, and her hair dancing in the air. I could feel the energy flowing around us. Elwin was standing not far away from her, smiling.

"What is she doing?" I asked when I was close enough.

He turned towards me and slightly bowed his head before answering.

"A beauty, isn't it? She's casting a protective spell on the castle."

My jaw dropped at this statement.

I asked in disbelief, "A protective spell around the whole castle, all by herself?"

Elwin grinned at my question.

"Impressive, right? She truly is a powerful witch."

I stood by Elwin's side, watching in awe as energy flowed from Ravynne. I felt grateful for her help. It was a blessing to have her with us.

After a moment, Ravynne stopped casting her magic. The wind surrounding us died. Panting, she fell to her knees. Elwin and I rushed to her side.

"Are you okay?" asked Elwin.

She nodded, still catching her breath.

"It's done," she whispered.

"Let's get her to the bench under the oak tree." I told Elwin.

He nodded. We helped her stand, each of us supporting an arm. We slowly walked with her towards the bench. The shade of the tree provided a nice spot to rest.

"I can't express how grateful I am for your help," I told Ravynne.

Her eyes lightened, and she smiled at my comment.

"It's nothing, really. Just doing my part to help, my Queen."

"You should rest here," I suggested.

Elwin added, "I'll stay with her until she's fine."

I nodded to them and walked around the courtyard.

I loved the fact that our soldiers were eating and joking together in the wait for the next wave. I was happy to see them relaxing and having fun despite everything. Even those foreign fighters, Cain and Zarek, were blending with the others.

The dragons were lying a little further. A few soldiers were trying to approach them warily, not knowing if it was safe to be near them or not. The dragons didn't seem to care. They let the curious soldiers get close to them.

Cara was lying by Ladon's side. Her head was intertwined with Ladon's heads. His tail was curled up around her, keeping her close to him. It looked as if he was hugging her. It was beautiful to see how much they loved each other. It got me thinking, "I wish Damien was here with me."

Just as I was thinking about that, I turned around and caught a glimpse of Elwin, holding Ravynne's hand, while sitting on the bench. He was smiling at her as they talked. I never thought this old vampire could show this much care and tenderness towards someone. It was heartwarming to see how love can strike you, no matter your age.

The ground suddenly shook, making the walls of the castle shake and dust fall to the ground. It was followed by a deep rumble. I tried to grab onto something, but there was nothing nearby. I lost my balance, falling to my knees on the ground. Fortunately, my hands stopped my fall, preventing me from hurting myself.

This wasn't good. I didn't know what caused this, but it made the hair stand up on the back of my neck. I looked around. Everyone was looking everywhere, trying to figure out what had just happened. All that I knew, was that it couldn't be a good thing. I had a very bad feeling about it.

I didn't have the time to think about it before one of the soldiers in the watch tower screamed, "They're coming! Prepare yourself!"

Soldiers started to run in every direction, grabbing weapons and shields, getting to their position. The dragons took flight, preparing to defend us from the air. Elwin and Ravynne hurried inside the castle. They had to prepare beds in the infirmary to accommodate the soldiers who would be injured.

Damien rushed to my side, a worried look on his face. He picked me up from the ground and grabbed me in his arms.

"Hurry, you must get inside, my little wolf."

As much as my wolf wanted to fight the enemy, I knew he was right. I needed to focus on myself and the baby. We got back inside the castle together.

Chapter 5 (Eurynomos)

Dark Temptation

Finally, the main portal was open! A few goblins died in doing so, but they were expendable. I was finally free to travel to the world of the livings. However, my powers were still lessened. I needed to restore them. I needed to find a vessel to do so. Preferably, a powerful one.

Two low-level demons barged into my room with a panicked look on their faces.

"You'd better not ruin my day," I warned them.

They glanced at each other nervously.

"Well...," started one.

He was hesitating and it was getting on my nerves.

"Spit it out, already!"

They shriveled in fear.

The same demon continued fearfully, "It seems that the werewolf is here. He found a way to get on the ferry. He's on his way right now."

He put his arm protectively in front of him after speaking. I growled at them. I didn't need any further delays. This had taken enough time already.

Sending my energy forward, I scanned my domain. I sensed his life force coming towards me. He wasn't that far and would arrive quickly. He was strong, but not strong enough. But more importantly, he was alone. That stupid wench wasn't here. She wasn't with him. Which meant this stupid mortal couldn't do anything against me.

The two lower demons in front of me were still waiting for my orders.

"I will deal with this impudent fool when he gets here. Prepare our fighters."

They nodded and hurried out of my palace. I would crush this idiot. Then I would get on with restoring my powers.

*********** Will's POV ***********

A deep rumble shook the ground. I had no idea what it was, but it came from the large structure where Eurynomos was, probably. I had no intention of waiting to discover what it was. As the boat docked to the shore, the souls started to get off.

Charron smiled wickedly at me.

He spoke with a twisted tone, "I wish I could witness myself what fate holds for you."

I only stared at him and got off the boat, a shiver running down my back.

I walked towards the dark structure. It looked like a dark tower surrounded by a shroud of dark cloud. The top of the tower had pointed tips that all carried a glowing blue flame. An evil aura seemed to emanate from it, making the air heavy and suffocating as I approached it. Orcs and lower demons tried to attack me. I quickly disposed of them. They were of no challenge to me. Now that I was closer to the tower, it looked bigger than I thought it would be. I pushed the heavy metal door and got inside.

I got to a long, dark hall. At the end of it, was a large room. A chandelier hung from the inter-sected patterns filling the ceiling. A big bookcase filled the left wall, with a few chairs to sit in while you read. A strange portal was anchored to the ground with bronze pillars.

At the end of the room, were two thrones. The biggest one was empty. I clenched my fists as I realized it must have been Eurynomos's throne. That bastard didn't deserve to have one. The smaller one had someone sitting lazily across it.

I took a step further. I watched in awe as what I could only describe as an angel flew to the air. What was an angel doing here? She wore a tight red dress decorated with silver threads. Her wings were black, embedded with red jewels. Her skin was pale, and her hair was as black as her eyes. She was definitely an angel. But I wasn't to be deceived. I could see her soul with my inner Alpha power. It was dark and powerful.

She got in front of me, her wings spreading wide, her feet almost touching the ground.

"Well, well. What do we have here?" she asked in a wicked tone.

"Get out of my way," I snarled. "I have things to settle with Eurynomos."

Her pointy teeth showed as she smirked and licked her lips.

"Hm…" she breathed out. "I don't think he'd like the likes of you bothering him. He's rather busy, you see."

The way her face lit up at the thought of the demon disgusted me.

I spat angrily, "You should be ashamed to have fallen into the graces of such a filthy demon."

She laughed heartily at my comment, the sound of her voice resonating through the walls.

"Oh, wolf boy… If only you knew how much I enjoy his grace." Her eyes gleamed with lust as she spoke those words.

A loud growl escaped my chest. She was a disgrace to her race.

"You're disgusting."

She feigned being offended.

"That's not a nice thing to say, little wolf. That's not how you should treat a lady."

I snarled at her, "I will put an end to your misery."

I ran towards her while she ran towards me as well. I swung my sword at her while she scratched me with her sharp nails. It hurt more than it should. A strange feeling started to fill me and forced me to breathe heavily.

I grunted, "What the hell is that?"

She smiled wickedly.

"Just a small perk I gained when I drank the demon's blood. That poison should help get rid of you faster."

My eyes widened when she said 'poison.' I didn't know how potent it was. It was slowing me down, but I wouldn't let it stop me.

I swung my sword at her unprotected neck. Fast as lightning, she stopped the blade with her bare hands. My blade didn't even scratch her. I fought to keep the blade at her neck, but she was pushing against it with such force. She finally got the blade off her neck, to the side.

She spoke with insolence, "You're going to have to do better than that, wolf boy."

She was taunting me, toying with me.

She charged at me, sending ribbons of black energy towards me. I had no idea how she was able to do so. Holes appeared in the floor where her ribbons landed as I was barely able to avoid them. The poison coursing through my veins was slowing me. I jumped, trying to attack from above. She jumped too, helped by her wings, and met me in the air. She sent a wave of energy towards me as I swung my blade at her. My blade was able to pass through her energy. However, the tip of the sword hardly scratched her cheek. Black blood was dripping from the mark it made.

She charged at me with her whole body. Tiles were kicked into the air and pain ripped through my back as I crashed to the floor, the angel's body weighing down on me. Pushing with all my force, I was able to swing us around, getting on top of her. Flapping her wings, she was able to push me back and fly away a little further.

She winced. She put her hand to her bleeding cheek.

"That hurt. What the hell did you do to me?"

I grinned at her comment.

"I guess it's the sacred sword, reacting to your vile demonic blood."

Her eyes widened and I couldn't help but laugh, happy to know my blade was effective against her. She launched herself at me again, but I was able to avoid her. She kept attacking me, and I kept avoiding her, but I was slowing down. I could feel the poison making its way through my veins. My vision became blurry for a moment before coming back. I felt my stomach churn. My wolf was trying to fight the poison, but he was already wounded from the mate bond severing. I needed to finish this fast, or my body would betray me.

I swung my sword at her. She screamed as I succeeded in slashing her breast. Blood started to drip from it, staining her dress. I was hoping that the sacred sword somehow had a weakening effect on her. She sent another wave of black energy ribbons at me, but I easily avoided them this time. The ribbons crashed into the bookshelf, sending books and paper flying through the air. I was sure she was slowing down. It was my chance to get the upper hand.

I jumped through the next wave of energy ribbons she sent me and managed to get close to her. Quickly, I stabbed my blade with force in her gut, dragging the sword upward. Her eyes opened wide, and she froze, surprised by the sudden pain ripping through her body. A single shriek of pain escaped her lips. I watched her lifeless body fall to the floor. Black blood pooled around her body.

I panted from the effort. I could still feel the poison coursing through my veins. The room was filled with dust and debris from our fighting. In the air lingered the smell of torn pages and blood. Black feathers lingered on the floor everywhere.

A black light emerged from the dead angel's body, followed by a pure, blinding white light. I wondered if she was forgiven for her sins, or if she would be damned for eternity.

A slow clap got me out of my thoughts. I looked up from the angel's body to see a tall black demon standing in front of me. He was taller than me. I could feel how powerful he was. The air crackled around him, filled with power. I could look at his soul. It was huge and darker than anything I'd seen in the past. Rage filled me when I realized that this was Eurynomos.

"Impressive, for a mere mortal," he spoke with a disgusted voice before looking at the angel's body on the floor. "Too bad. She was so good to fuck."

Bile filled my mouth at the thought of this vile demon fucking an angel. Or with anything… I couldn't imagine anyone wanting to fuck a demon.

I spat at him, "Shut up you murderer."

"Already with the big accusations… I'm not the one who killed Amaliel."

I growled at him, "No, but you're the one who killed my mate."

The demon smiled wickedly.

"Once again, I need to say that I wasn't the one to sink a sword into her."

My wolf flickered in anger at that statement, and a growl escaped my chest. I couldn't think straight anymore. I rushed towards him with the sacred sword. Eurynomos didn't even move. He blocked my blow without even lifting a finger. I kept launching blow after blow, desperate to kill my lover's killer, but I couldn't get one single strike at him. One strike did hit him on the arm, but he didn't even flinch.

I kept slashing with the sword, despair filling me as it became obvious that I couldn't kill him. Why? Why was fate so cruel? To have my mate taken away from me, and to be unable to kill the one responsible for her death. I kept fighting until I was panting from the effort. My lungs were burning.

Every muscle in my body was aching. I was barely able to move anymore. My earlier wounds from other battles and the poison started to take their tolls on my body.

Everything I did to get here… Was it all for nothing? I felt so useless. I cursed at the demon. Everything I knew. Everything was a lie. This life was a lie. The gods, if they even existed, were a lie. There was no justice in this world. Only pain and suffering. I would forever be tormented by the death of my mate, and my incapacity to avenge her. This realization hit me stronger than anything, hurting me to the depths of my soul.

"Are you done, now?" asked Eurynomos in a childish voice. "Poor little mortal… So frail, so useless!"

He approached me and touched my arm. I tried to get it away from him but could barely move it.

"What does it feel like? To be the murderer of the woman you loved."

"I didn't murder her!" I screamed with what little energy I had left.

Eurynomos tutted in annoyance.

"Enough with the lies, already! You murdered her, just as you murdered this one laying on the floor."

I looked at the angel's body. It was true. I did kill her. How many had I killed recently? Did the fact they were orcs and goblins justify the fact that I killed them? Did it make it okay because they were the bad guys? In their eyes, I was the bad guy. What would my mother think if she saw me right now? My hands were tainted with blood. I could never get them clean.

"Now then, I have a way for you to be useful."

"I want nothing from you, you wretched demon!"

"Now, hear me out before saying no. I could help you do what you couldn't. With my powers, you could revive your sweet Leila. You could hold her in your arms and kiss her again."

My heart stopped beating at this revelation. Was he speaking the truth? Of course, he wasn't. He was trying to deceive me. That's what demons did. I tried to move again, but my body felt sluggish.

"You lie! Stop talking and kill me already, as I can't get out of here."

"You!" Eurynomos shouted at a goblin hiding in a corner.

He cautiously approached, staring at me and the demon warily.

"Open a portal to the sacred grove of Ares, to the room where the girl lies."

He nodded nervously. "Yes, master."

I watched slowly as the goblin recited some words. A tear opened into reality, opening a window, allowing me to watch the sacred grove of Ares. Orcs were in the room, bashing everything they could. The roof was partly fallen, big boulders laying on the ground. There, at the center of the room, exactly where I left her, was Leila. Her lifeless body laid on the floor in a pool of blood. She was as pretty as she ever was. My wolf howled in pain at the sight of his mate. Tears started to roll down my cheeks.

"You fucking bastard!" I growled in anger. "Why do you insist on torturing me?"

Eurynomos shook his head.

"Don't you see what you could do with my power? We could retrieve her body while it's still intact. We could revive her. You only need to say it. Isn't that what you want to do, wolf-boy?"

I stared at him. I had no force left in my body; my mind felt clouded. Could he really be speaking the truth?

Chapter 6 (Bianca)

Ye Olde Atelier

We made it back to the city streets. We started to wander, looking at the shops and the houses. I wasn't sure where the magic guild was, but I was sure I'd recognize it once I'd seen it. People were still curious about us, but word of the battle from earlier had started to spread. Children would run by us out of curiosity as we made our way through the streets. I felt that our presence was more accepted than before. A flock of doves flew over our heads, and I wondered if it was a good luck omen.

We arrived at a town square. There was a large fountain in the center and some benches where people could sit in the shade of the trees. A musician was playing the flute. People were crowded around him to hear his song. We stopped for a while, listening to his beautiful melody. Kids were dancing near him, and people were happy. The musician's music was an oasis away from worries of the war. I let my troubles away for a moment, carried along by the music and the happiness of the moment. Steven twirled me to the sound of the music. A small girl grabbed my hand, and I danced with her too. Laughter filled the air; joy filled my heart. The musician bowed after finishing his song, as the crowd cheered for him.

He addressed to the crowd, *"Mërhank yôou.*[11]*"*

The elvish language sounded like a melody too. I wish I could learn it. Maybe when this war is over, I'd take the time to learn it. I could always ask Elashor. We left the town's square as the crowd dispersed.

We quickly made it to a street that was filled with shops. Each building had a different color, and some of them had apartments on top of the shopping floor. There were all kinds of shops, ranging from toy stores to armor shops. They were all stacked one against the other in a row.

The ground started to shake, forcing us to stop walking, a deep rumble rising everywhere around us. People were staring at each other, unsure

---

[11] Thank you.

of what was going on. I watched everyone. I knew from the deepest of my soul that this couldn't be good.

I said to the others, "I don't like the sound of this."

They nodded to me.

"Yes, we'd better find the magic guild, and fast," answered, Steven.

An old elven woman approached us slowly.

"Excuse me," she spoke with a slight accent. "Are you looking for the magic guild?"

I smiled at her.

"You speak English!"

"Yes, I've had the chance to learn it years ago when I traveled the lands. But that was a long time ago."

"That sounds amazing!" I replied. "And yes, we are looking for the magic guild."

She pointed to a street nearby.

"Just go a little further down that street. To the left, you will see it. You'll recognize it."

"Thank you so much!" I answered, excitedly.

She nodded and continued her path. People had returned to their daily lives as we walked further down the street that the lady had pointed to, looking for the magic guild.

We didn't need to walk very far before seeing it. The building was taller than most of the shops around. On each side of the big double-sided wooden door stood two tall statues of mages each holding a staff. A big circle decorated the doors. Inside the circle was a drawing of each phase of the moon. Around that big circle were twelve smaller circles with the symbol of each type of magic: fire, water, earth, ice, holy, dark, summoning, necromancy, alteration, restoration, transmutation, illusion.

"Huh, I'm surprised to see fire, water, earth and ice as separated types," I spoke out loud.

Arius replied, "Most of the time they are grouped under the term 'elemental magic.' But here, you can specialize in each element enough that they are considered a type in their own right."

I sucked in a breath at this thought. The mages here must be very powerful in order to achieve such a feat. I was hoping that someone would be able to help me harvest the magic of the Moon Goddess within me. The wooden door creaked softly as I pushed it open.

In front of us was a small wooden desk. Books and sheets of paper piled everywhere on it. A quill floated in the air, as a small elf was magically controlling it. He was scribbling something on the sheets of paper.

The wood elf didn't even raise his eyes from his work as he asked, "What can I do for you?"

"I need some magic training," I answered.

He spoke nonchalantly, "Guild registration number and name, please."

"Hum, I'm not registered with the guild."

The man raised a brow and glanced at me over his small round glasses that stood on the tip of his nose. He looked surprised to see that I wasn't an elf.

"I'm sorry, but I'm afraid that you need to be registered with the guild in order to benefit from our training."

I sighed. "I am the daughter of the Moon Goddess. I need training if I am to have any chance of defeating Eurynomos."

His eyes grew wide, and the quill that was floating fell to the desk, staining some documents with ink spots. The elf groaned at his ruined documents before looking back at me.

"Well, now. This is something I don't hear every day. Either you're desperate for training, or you're telling the truth. In which case, Iain would be very mad at me for not bringing your request to his attention."

"Iain?"

"The guild's high mage. Please, come with me."

We followed him to a big staircase. Blake whined at the number of floors we needed to go up.

He muttered, "You'd think they'd have magical stairs or something…"

"What was that?" asked the clerk.

"Nothing," answered, Blake.

We climbed the stairs all the way up to the highest floor. When we arrived at the top, we saw a tall high elf casting a spell. A book was floating in front of him as he recited the words from it. His long white hair was flying in the air, glowing yellow from the spell. His red plated mage robe was flowing around him. We watched in awe, waiting for him to be done with his spell.

The wind died when he stopped casting. The book rested on the pedestal. His hair and robe fell back down.

He turned towards us and spoke to the clerk, annoyed.

"I told you not to disturb me while I cast a spell."

The clerk stuttered, "I… I'm sorry high mage. This girl here claims to be the daughter of the Moon Goddess. I thought you'd want to see her."

The mage approached me, studying me with interest.

"Is that so? Huh…" He closed his eyes and opened his palm towards me. A soft wind flowed on my skin as he did. "I can sense a powerful amount of magic in you."

He opened his eyes again. "Who are you?"

"My name is Bianca. I am the Moon Goddess's daughter."

"I thought it was only a legend. Yet here you stand in front of me. What can I do for you?"

"Please, sir, I need your help. I need to learn how to control my magic power if I'm to succeed in killing Eurynomos."

The mage laughed.

"I'm not old enough to be called 'sir.' Call me Iain. You want to kill a demon?"

I nodded to him. "Yes, Iain. This demon is threatening to kill everyone and to rule over everything."

Iain laughed again. "You know, I was once married to a demon. If you knew my ex-wife, you'd believe this Eurynomos isn't so bad."

"Please, Iain, you must train me."

He gestured with his hand.

"Okay, fine. I will train you. What have we got here?" he asked, pointing to my friends.

Everyone presented themselves. Iain was curious about vampires.

"I've never seen vampires up close. This is interesting… I would love to study this curse of yours."

He asked, pointing to Steven, "So, you say this young man is your mate? And that he's a were-wolf?"

I nodded to him as Steven grabbed my hand in his, squeezing it lovingly.

"Brilliant! I love werewolves! I always wished I could be one. I could always transform myself into a wolf with magic, but I would never be able to experience the feeling of having a wolf living inside of me."

He took Steven's hand in his, turning it to each side, studying.

He mumbled to himself, "You can't even see the paws and where the claws retract. Interesting! I wonder if I can communicate with the wolf…"

It was clear he held werewolves in great awe.

I asked, breaking Iain's gaze as he examined Steven, "When can we start the training?"

He looked at me, smiling.

"Yes! Why not right away?"

I was happy. The sooner the better.

"That's great!" answered Zach. "Then we'll go and explore the city while you train."

I nodded to them. "That sounds like a great idea."

Steven grabbed my hips and kissed me lovingly. I love him so much.

He whispered, "I'll be back later, my love."

I watched as my friends left the room with the clerk, leaving me alone with the Iain. I had no idea what this training would be like, but I had a feeling it would be hard. It didn't matter. I would do whatever it took to master my powers and defeat Eurynomos.

************ Blake's POV ************

We exited the magic guild. I was quite impressed with the guild. A few students seemed to be strong. I could sense their magic aura right when we entered the building. I glimpsed powerful relics exposed behind a magical protective field. And Iain looked very powerful. Surely, he would be able to teach Bianca to master her powers.

"Think there's anything of interest in this city?" asked Steven.

"Of course!" answered Arius. "This is the biggest elven city! We're bound to find something worth our time."

We passed a few shops. I was impressed by the richness of the elvish culture and history.

"I can't believe I lived almost two centuries without ever visiting this place!" I spoke, admiring the architecture. Nobody said anything, but I knew they agreed with me.

We soon came to a weird-looking shop called "Ye Olde Atelier."

"What the hell is that shop?" Zach asked.

Looking through the window, we could see all kinds of weird contraptions.

"There's only one way to find out!" I answered, opening the door, and getting inside the shop.

The light dimly entered the shop through the window. The store was filled with a various number of things, ranging from metal statues to strange jewelry of all sizes. There were weird machines and tools, a few hammers made from different metals. Weird clocks hung on the wall. The walls themselves had mechanisms moving, and I wondered what purpose they served. Some gizmos were moving, their mechanisms turning as the machine moved. Others had levers and buttons. I had to refrain from pressing them, as I was curious to see what it did.

A small man cleared his throat from behind the counter. I looked up at the counter to see a man barely above it. I was surprised to see a dwarf in this elven city. His glasses sat on his round nose. He had a thick red beard and wore a brown bowler hat. His bulky hands sat atop the counter.

We walked up to the counter, and I realized he was standing on a stool. He looked like he was four feet at most.

I spoke first, "Good day, my good sir."

"Well, good day to you," he answered with a croaky voice. "What can I do for you?"

"I have to say, we were quite intrigued with your shop, and decided to have a look inside."

He smiled at my statement.

"Ah! Yes! This is my knick-knack shop. Kõrvits, inventor of things, at your service."

He removed his hat as he said this, showing his short red hair.

"Inventor?" Elashor asked in surprise.

"Why, yes, my young lady! Would you like to hear more about it?"

"We do have some free time at the moment," answered, Steven. "I would love to hear all about it."

Kõrvits rubbed his hands together, smiling.

"Then, might I interest you in a cup of coffee or tea? I bought a delicious pumpkin pie this morning but didn't have the time to eat it yet."

I smiled.

"Sure!"

The dwarf pulled on a lever, and the gears in the walls started to turn. A trapdoor in the ceiling opened, and a staircase began to descend. The gears stopped moving when the staircase reached the floor.

We were all looking at him with our mouths agape.

Kõrvits smiled. "Impressive, isn't it?"

He gestured for us to follow him up the stairs. The second floor held a kitchenette with a round table. We were inside the roof of the shop. Big windows allowed us to admire the city from up there, giving a nice view of the surroundings. I was surprised to see that many shops had a small terrasse on their roofs. One of the windows was open, letting the sound of birds and a gentle breeze enter the room.

"Please, take a seat," said the dwarf as he prepared tea and coffee.

The table was too low for us to use the chairs. We decided to sit with crossed legs on the floor. Kõrvits brought drinks and pumpkin pie to everyone and came to sit with us.

"So, you're an inventor?" asked Elashor, her eyes sparkling with curiosity.

"Ah! Yes, my young lady."

"Elashor."

"Right, Elashor. I was once an adventurer."

"You were?" I asked, intrigued.

"Indeed, I was. I used to travel the lands with a group of dwarves. We used to explore ancient ruins in the search of riches and to help people who needed us."

"What did you do to help people?" asked Elashor.

"Oh, all kinds of things! Kill some rats, fetch rare items, or kill reported monsters."

She gasped.

"Kill some monsters?"

"Yes! That, and catching scoundrels and robbers."

"That sounds like it was a good life," commented Arius.

"It was! That's when I discovered I wasn't good at fighting. But I was good at making things that fought for me."

"That fought for you?" I asked, intrigued.

The old dwarf grinned.

"Yes, I invented countless flying machines, catapults, and robots. They fought enemies alongside my friends. It was my way of helping them."

"That sounds ingenious," I commented.

"Then why aren't you doing it anymore?" asked Steven.

Kõrvits' face changed.

"One day, we were tracking a gang of bandits that were terrorizing a small village to the East. We had heard they were hiding in a cave nearby. We set up camp a mile away from there to plan our attack."

His eyes were staring at the empty space, watching memories from another time that only he was able to see.

"We were ambushed at night by the bandits. I woke up to my friends being massacred by them. I hid in the bushes, as I couldn't fight them. My robots weren't ready to fight either. I hadn't had the time to prepare them. I watched in horror as they killed each of my friends. When they left, I ran away as far as I could until I arrived in this city."

We all sat in silence, taking in his sad story.

"When I arrived here, I was feeble, tired, and my soul was destroyed from the loss of my friends. The city was open to everyone. I found people who welcomed me, gave me a home, a family, and friendship. When I felt better, I decided to stay here, and do what I did the best. Be an inventor."

Silence filled the room as we thought about what Kõrvits had just said. It must have been hard. But it was good that he found a way to feel better.

"I thought dwarves hated elves," spoke Elashor.

Kõrvits grinned. "It's true, there are some old quarrels between dwarves and elves. But I've lived here for almost a hundred years now. Helped countless people and built true friendships. Whatever old quarrels existed; they're forgotten."

Elashor said out loud what we all thought, "I think it's wonderful that you found a place to live happily."

"Why didn't you go back?" asked Steven.

"Back where?" asked Kõrvits. "To adventure?"

"No," Steven replied. "To your dwarven city."

"I thought about it a few times," admitted Kõrvits. "The city I'm from lies very far away from here. It would take several weeks for me to travel there. I don't want to be the bearer of bad news. I don't want to be the one to tell about my friend's deaths. I'd rather they believe we're still having an adventure."

I could relate to him. Imagine, being the only one of the group to make it back to your hometown. Having to explain to everyone how they got killed. Having to justify why you're still alive when everyone else is dead. I bet he felt guilty behind his facade of a friendly joker.

"Enough chatting, this pie is not going to eat itself!" declared Kõrvits.

We ate the pumpkin pie he had given us.

"This is really good," I said surprised, as pumpkin is not usually my favorite.

Kõrvits smiled. "They baked it especially for me at the bakery down the street. Pumpkin is my favorite."

I made a mental note to visit that bakery later. If they could turn pumpkin into something that delicious, then surely, they were able to do wonders with other things.

We thanked Kõrvits for the coffee and pie and got back down to the shop.

"Before you go," he called after us.

He gave a small pocket watch to Elashor.

"Please take this."

She looked at it from all angles.

"It's a pocket cuckoo clock."

"A what?" she asked him.

"A pocket cuckoo. I made it myself. The cuckoo strikes the hour."

We watched the small pocket watch, not bigger than a hand.

"It must be very small!" Elashor commented.

Kõrvits grinned. "It was hard to do, but I'm pretty proud of it."

Elashor hugged the old dwarf. "Thank you so much!"

"Well, until next time!" He waved at us as we exited the shop.

We walked in the street and ended up back at the fountain without even realizing it. Elashor got the pocket clock out just as three o'clock hit. Sure enough, a small mechanical cuckoo made it out of the watch to strike the hour.

"Well, what do you know?! That's impressive!" commented Zach.

We all agreed.

"Why don't we stop for a break?" asked Elashor. She sat on a bench with Arius. Soon after, they were kissing.

"Why don't we regroup at five in front of the magic guild?" proposed Zach. "I'll go check the local weapon shop."

"Wait for me!" Steven added eagerly.

I nodded to them.

"You guys go ahead. I want to see that bakery Kõrvits was talking about."

We let Arius and Elashor have some time alone. I guess they didn't get a lot of chance to be by themselves, lately. I'm sure they would appreciate some privacy… even if it was in a public square in front of a fountain.

I walked back to the same street we had come from, passed Kõrvits' shop, and eventually came by a small bakery. The smell of fresh bread came from the doors as clients entered the shop. Through the window, I could see multiple bakeries and cakes. They even had specialty pastries we only have in vampire bakeries. Although we usually made them with blood. I highly doubted these had any blood in them. But I was surprised, nonetheless.

Just as I was about to enter the bakery, the door opened, and Eshenesra came out of the bakery. I froze, unable to move, struck by her beauty. She was carrying baskets of breads and pastries. It was heavy, and she was struggling to carry them all.

She froze and stared at me. Her yellow eyes were staring into my soul. She truly was a black diamond, just waiting to be picked. The only thing I could think of was how much I wanted to get close to her, to sink my teeth into her neck, and kiss her.

"Hi," I spoke, not really knowing what to tell her. "I, huh, saw you this morning at the palace."

She was watching the ground, not answering anything.

"I… I'm sorry for what happened. That was clumsy of me… I'm sorry."

I frowned at her sentence.

"What are you talking about? What happened wasn't your fault."

Her eyes rose to look into mine for an instant. I could read untold secrets in them.

"P… please, it was…"

"It wasn't!" I shouted.

She took a step back, and I immediately felt bad for screaming at her. I didn't want to frighten her. I just got so mad thinking back to what had happened.

"I'm sorry I shouted." I only hoped she would forgive me. She just stood there, watching.

"That manager, he's the one responsible. He had no right to talk to you the way he did. You shouldn't let him yell at you like that."

I wished she would open up to me. I wanted her to answer anything. But she didn't. I had no way of knowing what she thought. She only stared at the ground.

Not knowing what to say next, I asked, "Do you need help to bring all of those to the palace?"

She answered in a small voice, "I don't want to bother you."

"It's not bothering me at all," I answered happily as I grabbed the basket. It was easy for me to carry it, and I was happy to help her.

I started walking in the direction of the palace, with her by my side. I was enjoying her closeness. I had until the palace to try to make her talk a little bit. Or to find something to say. I felt clumsy near her. It's like the words stumbled inside of me and I couldn't form a coherent sentence. I only hoped she would make conversation with me.

Chapter 7 (Eshenesra)

The Sleeping Queen

He was so strong. He was able to lift the baskets so easily. Why was he so nice to me? I was just a palace servant. What's more, only a dark elf. No one liked dark elves. That's why our kind were so reclusive. Yet, here he was, helping me. I didn't know how to react to kindness. It wasn't something people usually show around me.

He was so close to me as we walked to the palace. His body was colder than mine. I guessed he was a vampire. I thought I'd be scared the first time I met a vampire. Yet, here I was, thrilled to be so close to him. All those thoughts raced through my mind. Would he drink my blood if he got the chance? Were all vampires blood sucking murderers? Could they really be trusted?

I was sure the reputation of their race was exaggerated. A little bit like the reputation of dark elves. But I couldn't get past the fact they drank blood to sustain themselves.

"You can answer when I ask you a question."

I looked at him, surprised. I was so lost in my thoughts; I wasn't paying attention to what he was saying.

"I'm really sorry, huh… I don't know your name," I admitted.

"Blake," he answered in a deep voice.

His voice sounded sexier than I wanted to admit.

"I'm sorry, Blake. I was lost in my thoughts."

His smile warmed my heart. I didn't want to give in to those feelings. Love only ended in deception and hurt. I didn't understand why I was attracted to him, but it was better that I forget about him. He would surely leave the city when he finished his business here. Then I'd go back to being the servant I was always at the palace. Alone and forgotten by everyone.

"I wanted to know what your job is at the palace."

"I'm of no interest. I only make food and clean the palace."

Blake smiled at my answer.

"I would love to taste the food you prepare."

I felt my cheeks reddening from his compliment. It made me happy to know he would love to taste my food. Nobody ever said anything about the food I make.

"So, do you have family or friends around here? I didn't see a lot of dark elves in the city."

My heart sank at his question. I didn't want to tell him how my family was brutally murdered. I didn't want to admit how I missed them every day, even if it's been decades. I skipped this part and chose to answer about the dark elves only.

"Most of the dark elves live in hiding. My race is not appreciated by the other races. For years, we've been persecuted. Because of that, many of us became what the other accused us of being: assassins and criminals. Very few of us live in the city. Those who do, live in hiding."

Blake frowned at my comment.

"People shouldn't judge others based on their races. This is stupid."

He was right. But the context and our history turned people's minds in an irreversible way.

He added, "I guess that when you're told so many times that you're bad, it changes you, and you become what they say."

I smiled at him.

"Thanks, you're so nice to me."

He looked at me with such a smile that I wanted to hide below the cobblestones we were walking on. I fiddled nervously with my fingers.

"Do you have a family?"

Again, with this question. I sighed. I guess I had to answer something…

"No, they were all killed when I was a child."

His face changed at this sentence.

"I'm very sorry."

I could feel he was sincere. It was a strange feeling to have someone being nice to me. I could get used to that. But I knew he would probably leave in a few days. I would be crushed if I got attached to him.

As we got to the palace, Blake turned to me and said, "I'll accompany you up to where you need to bring those."

I was grateful for his help. I only hoped Scalanis wouldn't be mad at me for having someone helping me. We made our way towards the servant's quarters.

As I opened the door, Scalanis immediately started swearing at me.

"There you are, Eshenesra. You good-for-nothing wench! You took your sweet time. Who's going to wipe the floors while you're away? I should teach you a lesson."

He turned my way and froze when he saw Blake. Blake seemed to be boiling with anger.

He put the basket on the table without saying anything. He took a few steps towards Scalanis, looking like he would rip his head off. Scalanis gulped down and stepped back. I couldn't help but to rejoice at the sight of this mean elf that I hated so much, being scared like that of Blake. After a few steps, Scalanis couldn't get further away, his back hitting the wall.

Blake spoke to him sternly.

"Let me make myself clear. The next time you talk to her this way, I will personally rip the tongue out of your mouth, so that you can't speak anymore. Do I make myself clear?"

Scalanis nervously nodded. I stood in the corner, trying to hide my smile.

Blake turned towards me, smiling.

"It was nice talking with you."

I smiled back at him.

"Thanks for your help," I answered shyly.

He waved at me. I watched as he exited. My treacherous heart was beating for him, despite me. I didn't want to get attached to him. But it was already too late for that.

*********** Will's POV ************

I stood back up. The power was flowing through my body. Never have I felt more powerful. I could feel the darkness coursing through my veins. The demon was staying silent, residing inside of me, sharing my body with my wolf. He was keeping his end of the bargain so far. I clenched my fists, trying to forget the pact I made with this vile demon to get my mate back. I couldn't live without her. I didn't care what needed to be done; I would get her back.

The goblin quivered in fear at my sight. I watched him with a cold stare. The only thing that mattered now was getting Leila's body while it was still intact. I made a step towards the portal, but the goblin stopped me with his staff, pearls of sweat beading on his forehead.

"You dare to stop me?" I roared at him, my voice echoing on the walls of the room.
The ground shook from my power.

"This… this portal is only an exit. You need to go through the main portal to be able to come back through it, master."

I grunted with annoyance.

"He is telling the truth," spoke Eurynomos through my mind. *"Get to the main chamber. The portal is there."*

"Show me the way to the main chamber," I ordered the goblin.

He nodded at my request, bringing me to a vast room a little further down. It was filled with magic trinkets, and a large portal stood at the center of the room.

I tried to get to the portal, but orcs barred the way.

"Can't you fools recognize your master when he's in front of you?" shouted Eurynomos through my mouth with a dark, deep voice.

I wasn't used to having my body controlled by someone other than me. It was weird to hear my voice sound like this.

The orcs stared at me, stunned, but let me through to the portal.

"How does this thing work, demon?" I asked out loud to Eurynomos.

"Just focus on where you want to go, and the portal will do the rest," the demon answered through my mind.

I focused my mind on the sacred grove of Ares, thinking of my sweet Leila and where her body was lying. Soon enough, the portal glowed, and it focused on where I wanted to go. Just as I tried to step into it, a centaur approached. He looked at me, confused, but then seemed to recognize the demon in me.

"I came to report on the war, sir."

Just as I was about to ignore him and step into the portal, Eurynomos stopped me.

"We need to continue the war. Hear him out," he ordered me through my mind.

I groaned in annoyance.

"Go ahead," I said sternly to the centaur.

"The invasion is going well. The massacre has started in all the big cities. Everything should be ready soon for your arrival."

The thought of people getting killed was sickening me. But I couldn't do anything about it for now. Not until I had my Leila back.

"Good, dismissed," I answered.

He looked at me, uneasy.

"What should we do next, sir?"

I shrugged my shoulder.

"You're the general, aren't you?"

The creature nodded.

"Then figure it out. I have more pressing matters," I spat as I took a step into the portal, determined to get to my beloved Leila.

An angry Eurynomos groaned inside of me.

He warned me, *"Be careful, wolf-boy. Remember our agreement."*

I spat back at him, "Don't you worry, demon. I shall not forget."

The orcs stared at me with their stupid stare as I exited the portal and appeared near Leila's body.

"What are you looking at?" growled Eurynomos through my mouth.

The orcs leaped in surprise and backed away when they recognized the demon.

I picked up Leila's body. She was so cold, bathed in blood. She was so pretty, despite being dead. My heart was tearing apart at seeing her like that. All the sadness I was trying to push away came flooding back. I hugged her lifeless body in my arms, trying to remind myself that soon she would be alive again by my side.

Would she hate me for what I'd done? Would she forgive me? Would she understand that I couldn't let her go? I only hope she would still love me, despite what I'd become.

The ground shook, and loose rocks fell from the ceiling. This whole place was threatening to fall; to crumble. Without waiting any longer, I stepped back into the portal, holding the woman I loved in my arms.

The underworld was inhospitable. I didn't want my sweet Leila to come back to life in this barren world. I had heard of the legend of Darton castle. It was supposed to be an old, abandoned castle, lost in the mountains to the North. That would be a better base than this wretched place.

"I'm getting away from this place," I grunted to the demon.

"We can't stop the invasion. Don't you forget our deal, or she will stay a corpse forever."

My wolf growled at the demon's threat.

I turned to the centaur general.

"You there, keep the invasion going. We need to get these cities under our control."

"Yes, sir."

"I need a small detachment to come with me. I'll need protection in my castle as I take care of Leila."

"Yes, master," answered another goblin.

People started to run everywhere, responding to the orders I gave. The centaur general came to see me, holding a small portal.

"Sir, while you're away, we'll be able to stay in touch with this portal. I'll be able to report to you, and you'll be able to send your orders."

This was exactly what I needed.

"Good." This will be more useful than I thought it would be.

I spoke low enough only for Eurynomos to hear, "Satisfied, demon?"

The demon growled in my chest, making me understand he was okay with this arrangement.

I looked at the portal and concentrated on everything I knew about Darton castle. I only hoped it would work, even though I didn't know its exact location. I focused for a long time, a blurry image forming on the portal. Yes, it was taking shape! I kept thinking about it. I could remember it now. I didn't understand why I could remember it.

"It's because I've been there before," spoke the demon in my mind.

Somehow, Eurynomos's memories and mine were blending. I didn't care, as it was proving to be quite useful.

After a while, a dark castle appeared on the portal. It stood on an icy mountain. The winds and snow were smashing against its walls. Its highest towers seemed lost in the dark clouds above. The windows were dark, and it gave the castle a gothic cathedral vibe. I would make sure to get this place lively again for Leila. Everything in its time.

I stepped into the portal with Leila's body still in my arms. I opened the big, heavy wooden door. The castle was dark, but I found that with my new powers, I only had to concentrate on the braziers for a flame to come alive. This new power was proving rather useful. The place was covered in spider webs and dust. In the air lingered a scent of mold. I walked into the throne room. That would be the perfect base for me.

"We need to get the portal in this room," I said to the demon inside of me.

He didn't answer, but I sensed a power coming from inside me. A few seconds later came the portal, floating in the air, pulled by my power. The portal stopped in front of the throne. As I concentrated on it, loose stones came floating from other rooms of the castle and assembled themselves to form a pedestal, firmly holding the portal in place.

"There," answered, Eurynomos.

I looked through the portal. The centaur general was still standing there.

"Are my troops ready?" I asked.

"Yes, sir, they're waiting for your orders."

"Good, make them come here. I need my battalion ready to defend this castle."

The centaur nodded. On the other side of the portal, rows of demons, succubi, harpies, centaurs, orcs, and goblins started to cross through the portal, making their way to the castle.

"Start by getting this place cleaned up," I ordered the first troops arriving. "I'll be back in a while to assess your progress."

They didn't argue. Only nodded and got to the task at hand.

I ventured into the castle in the search of a room suitable for my sweet Leila. I soon found exactly the room that I needed. It was still fairly intact. It was probably the Queen's room. The ceiling was decorated with painted golden roses. The windows were draped with rich dark red curtains with golden thread linings. A majestic bed occupied the wall at the back of the room. The bed was still made, as if someone had intended to come back to it. The sheets looked still intact and clean.

This room was perfect for my mate, my sweet Leila. I would make her my queen. I laid her on the bed and removed her blood-stained clothes. In the adjacent bathroom, I found a washcloth. I gently cleaned the blood off of her body with warm water. She was as beautiful as the day I first laid my eyes on her. The closet still had some women's clothes. I found a light-pink dress that suited her perfectly. I laid her gently under the covers. With her eyes closed, dressed like that, she almost looked like she was sleeping.

Even my wolf was fooled, begging me to get into bed with her and wake her up. But I knew her heart wasn't beating anymore, and her body was cold. I kissed her cool lips before stepping back from the bed.

"Demon, now's the time to hold your part of the bargain. Resurrect her!" I ordered Eurynomos.

The demon growled inside of me.

"Such impudence! I cannot resurrect her yet. My powers are not completely restored."

"What? You lied to me!" I shouted with rage.

"I will be able to resurrect her as soon as we retrieve the Desire's Etcher."

"What the hell is the Desire's Etcher?" I shouted anger boiling in my veins.

"Calm down, wolf-boy. It's the enchanted dagger owned by the Queen of the Air Nymphs. It holds the rest of my powers."

"You never said anything about this before."

"You didn't ask about it."

I cursed at the vile demon. I hated Eurynomos, but he was the key to seeing my sweet Leila again.

"Where can I find this Queen?"

"She resides on top of Nokorath Hills, south of the elven city Mytvathyr."

The ground shook around me from anger.

I stormed outside of the room and made my way back into the throne. My battalion was all there now. The room was cleaned. They looked at me with fear, sensing the rage I was in.

"Listen to me," I spat at them. "In the room in the back lies my mate. I will kill each and every

one of you if anything happens to her. Am I understood?"

They nodded nervously.

"In the meantime, you shall restore the rest
of the castle, and guard the entrance against attack-
ers."

"Yes, master," a succubus answered, bow-
ing lowly.

A gargoyle was waiting for me outside the
castle. It was tall, gray, and bony. It had no scales,
fur, or feathers. Only bare skin. It had sharp claws
on its arms that transformed into giant bat-like
wings. It had a long tail and had holes for a nose. It
looked at me with its sharp teeth and pointy ears. If
I had known I would fly on such a horrendous creature, I would have kept Ladon by my side, I mumbled to myself.

"You'd better not deceive me, demon," I
warned Eurynomos before mounting the creature.
The creature soon started to fly south, in the direction of the Nokorath Hills.

Chapter 8 (Bianca)

Royal Bath

Sweat beaded on my forehead. How many hours has it been since my friends left me? My mind felt hazed from the effort. I fell to my knees. I had been able to learn to control some of the elements. I felt like I wasn't learning fast enough, but Iain seemed to think otherwise.

"You're making great progress!"

I took a deep breath, my arms still shaking. I felt angry at myself for not being able to learn faster.

"I know, but I'm not ready yet."

"You're doing amazing! Most mages take months to learn what you learned today!"

"I haven't even started to learn how to control the Moon Goddess's powers!"

Iain smiled and held a hand to get me off the floor.

"The Moon Goddess's powers are very unique. You must learn to use basic magic before hoping to master more advanced techniques."

I knew he was telling the truth, but I still felt frustrated. I knew I had the power to heal people. I had done it multiple times before. But it had manifested itself when I needed it. I didn't control it. I even revived Damien once, for God's sake! But then, it had been the Moon Goddess spreading her powers through me. I wondered if I could be able to harness and control such a powerful power. I had no idea what destructive powers I would have against Eurynomos. All I knew was that centuries ago, the Moon Goddess defeated him. The legend didn't say how. I wish I could speak with her so that I could ask her. But she only spoke to me when she deemed it necessary. I couldn't initiate the conversation. I wish I could ask her for advice.

I stood up. All my body was hurting. I felt like I could collapse at any moment. My lungs felt like they were burning. But I didn't want to stop now.

I stared at Iain with a determined look.

"Okay, let's do this again."

I was bracing myself and concentrating. Iain started laughing.

"Oh, no! We're done for today, my young lady."

My mouth went agape. "What? Why?"

He shook his head. "Can't you feel how tired you are? Can't you see you've pushed yourself enough already?"

I protested, "But…"

Iain brushed my protests aside.

"I won't hear any excuses. Your body will crumble if you keep pushing."

He grinned as he added, "Besides, I have a date with a nice elf lady tonight. I wouldn't want to be late."

"What? But you can't go on a date when we have a demon to defeat."

"Now, now. I haven't met her yet. She might not be a demon." He laughed at his own joke.

I felt so frustrated. I wanted to train more, but it was evident we were done for today.

"We'll train tomorrow. In the meantime, you should rest. You need to get your strength back."

I sighed, "Okay, thank you Iain. You've been a great help!"

He smiled. "See you tomorrow, Bianca."

It's only when I went down the stairs that I truly understood how tired my body really was. It took all my strength to keep me from collapsing on the stairs. Just as I got to the last floor, the front door opened, and Blake entered. His black hair was tied in a low bun. I was surprised, as he usually wears it loose. He had a big smile.

"Hi Blake! What's got you so happy?" I asked him.

He raised a brow and smirked. "I don't know. I guess I'm just happy."

I walked towards him, but almost fell to the floor. He grabbed me before I hit the ground.

"Lucky, I came to see how you were doing."

I winced. "I guess I overdid it."

He laughed at my statement.

"That's one way to put it. Come on. Let's see if the others are coming back."

We exited the magic guild and found Arius and Elashor waving at us, walking hand in hand. They looked truly happy together. I was so glad that Arius has gotten a second chance at love. He deserved to be happy after everything his father put him through. I smiled as further back; I saw Zach and Steven having a lively conversation. Their hands were full of bags. We waited for them to reach us.

Steven's face changed when he saw that Blake was supporting me.

"Bianca! Are you alright?"

He rushed to me, letting his bags on the ground. Blake let go of me, and I fell into Steven's arms.

"I'm fine," I whispered into his neck. "I just overdid it a little."

He rolled his eyes. "Yeah, right. You '*over-did it a little*.' Don't kill yourself for training!"

I smiled at him. I was so glad he cared for me as much as he did.

Zach grinned. "We have something perfect for you!"

I looked at him with questioning eyes.

"We went to the blacksmith, the armorer, and magic supplies shop. Oh Bianca, you would have loved it! It was called Dragonborn."

"Talk about an awesome name for a shop!" added Steven.

I laughed. Steven looked like a child. I thought he looked so cute. I wondered if our children would look like him when we have some. Steven smirked at me at this thought.

He pushed through my mind, "I can't wait to find out."

I blushed, then spoke out loud to Zach. "Well, it looks like you two had some fun while I was working hard. So, what's perfect for me, then?"

Steven smirked. "Me! Of course!"

I laughed heartily. "I kind of already knew that!"

Zach smiled. "We found a nice mage's robe when we were at the Dragonborn. I'm not sure exactly what it does, but we figured it would be great for you."

"That, and the fact that the dress is powder blue, and will probably cling perfectly to your curves." Steven's eyes had a luscious spark to them.

"Okay, okay. Get a room you two," teased Arius.

"Right, didn't the Queen say we would have rooms made available at the castle?" asked Elashor.

"Right!" suddenly Blake spoke as if he just remembered something. "We're invited to eat with the King and Queen tonight. And yes, rooms have been made available for all of us."

"That's nice!" I exclaimed.

"Did you go to the palace this afternoon?" asked Arius. Blake smiled and nodded.

We all started to walk towards the palace. As we walked, a creature flew over our heads. It was enormous and laid a big shadow over the floor. It had huge bat-like wings. It was gray and bony. I had never seen anything like it.

"What the hell is that?" asked Elashor.

"More importantly, is that Will on the back of the creature?" asked Blake.

I watched in horror, and sure enough, I could see Will on the back of the creature.

"Will!" I tried to scream his name, but he didn't hear me.

"It's no use. He won't hear us. He's way too high up," Steven said.

"Where is he headed?" asked Elashor.

We looked at the creature flying south. "The only thing I know that's south of here, is the Nokorath Hills." Said Zach.

"You know this place?" asked Arius.

"Yeah, I heard some towns people talk about it while we were shopping," answered Zach. "I have no idea what's there, though."

I watched Will fly on the creature, a dark feeling creeping in my heart.

I whispered, "That looks like a problem."

Everyone nodded in silence. "Well, I think I'll skip the supper and head directly to Nokorath Hills," stated Zach.

"I'm coming too," added Arius, with a serious face.

"And so am I," added Elashor with a wink, before adding, "there's no way I'm letting you have all the fun without me."

"Good, then it's decided. Let's grab a quick lunch, then head to the mountain on our horses."

I protested, "Hey! I want to go too."

"You can barely stand on your own," Steven replied softly. I knew he was right, but I still felt guilty for the fact that Will's mate had been killed.

"And you need to be back to the magic guild tomorrow morning for further training," said Blake, before adding, "Let's get back to the palace. We wouldn't want to keep the King and Queen waiting."

Reluctantly, I nodded and followed them to the palace. My legs felt too weak to try to go against their advice. I was basically dragged by Steven. I knew my mate wouldn't let me do something that reckless, anyway. He knew the state I was in.

"Damn right! I won't leave your side until you feel better." He pushed through my mind.
His words were kind, but I could feel the resolve of his wolf. He would go to the end of the world for me.

"Thanks, my love." I pushed back into his mind. I immediately felt his wolf relax at those words.

As we arrived at the palace, Zach looked at Blake. "Please explain to the King and Queen that we can't be there for supper. We'll grab a meal from

the kitchen before heading out on our horses."
Blake nodded. I hugged them and wished them
well.

As we got inside the palace, Blake left to
speak with the King and Queen. A servant showed
us to our room.
I was amazed when I entered our bedroom.
There was a big bed on the back wall, and in front
of it was a fireplace. Wooden beams decorated the
ceiling. The floor was tiled with different kinds of
marble and stones, forming an elegant pattern. One
of the corners had a small table with two chairs.

I let myself fall on the bed, exhausted.
"Why don't you take a relaxing bath?" pro-
posed Steven. "I'm sure you'll feel better."
Every muscle in my body was aching.
"It sure sounds like a good idea."
Steven smiled, his wolf purring softly. "I'll
prepare the bath for you, my love."
He brushed a kiss on my lips before going to the
bathroom.

He came back a few seconds later. "The
water is pouring, and I added a few plants to the
water. It should help you relax and feel better."
His strong arms enveloped me, and my
body immediately relaxed. I took a deep breath of
his scent. He kissed my neck softly.
"We should probably get to the bathroom,"
I whispered.
He smirked and lifted me in his arms. I
hung on to his shoulders as he brought me to the
bathroom.

I was surprised at the size of the bathtub. It was probably big enough for three or four people. I guessed that was one of the perks of living in a castle. I'll have to remember to compare the baths in the vampire castle.

"I would love to visit your sister's castle's baths with you," a husky voice answered in my head.

I smiled as Steven gently put me on the ground. The bath was already more than half full. The whole room smelled like flowers.

I slowly removed my clothes. Steven's eyes were devouring my body while I did. I could feel his desire through our mate bond. I loved the power my body held over him. How this strong wolf would fall to his knees for me.

I moaned as my body got into the warm water. I immediately felt reinvigorated.
I heard clothes drop to the floor behind me. I turned around to see Steven naked.

He asked with a smile, "Can I join?"

I teased him, "Looks like you already decided."

He laughed and explained, "I didn't think you'd object."

I smirked and raised a brow. "What if I did?"

He chuckled lowly. "Look me in the eyes and tell me seriously that you don't want me in the bath with you."

"You know I do." He grinned and made his way into the water with me.

Steven started to wash my body, gently caressing my skin as he did. Shivers ran through my body as he kissed every inch of my skin. I loved how this strong man could take care of me so gently. The exhaustion I was feeling earlier was gone. My body was now yearning to get close to Steven's hard-muscled body. To fit with his body the way only my body could; so perfectly made for one another, in a bliss of love and pleasure. I kissed him languorously, pulling him closer to me.
A moan escaped my mouth as my nipples brushed on his chest. His wolf growled with desire through his chest. I knew how much he loved it. I could already feel his bulge building in the water between us.

"Oh, baby girl! Are you sure you can handle this? You were pretty exhausted earlier." I loved the fact he was concerned for me. I nodded, a devilish smile on my face.

"Damn, I love that sexy smile of yours!" His words rolled on my breast as he licked them with hunger. His fingers were worshipping every inch of my body. I couldn't hold a moan as he started to play with my clit. I started to thrust my hips, my pussy wet despite being in the bath. He kept rubbing my clit, pleasure was building up inside me.

"Oh, Steven! Take me!" I pleaded.

"Not before you cum for me, love."

He grabbed my hips with his other hand, holding me in place as he expertly rubbed my pussy. I arched my back, moaning loudly as I came.

His eyes sparkled with excitement. "You're so gorgeous!"

He inserted his finger into my opening, making me moan.

"Fuck, Steven! I came, take me."

"Turn around," he ordered.

His voice was full of authority. I knew it came from his wolf. I loved when his wolf took the best of him and took control. I turned around, kneeling in the bath, holding the edge of it.

"Now, cum again for me, love," he ordered as he entered me.

I moaned at the feeling of his hard cock filling me. He started thrusting his hips, waves forming in the bath as we made love. Water was spilling on the floor, but I couldn't care less. My body was quivering with pleasure as Steven thrust into me countless times. He kept thrusting into me, the hot breath from his groans blowing on my neck. I felt myself tighten around him as he thrust deeper. I couldn't hold myself back, screaming his name as I climaxed, my walls pulsing around him. He moaned hard as he came a few seconds later.

"Good girl," he whispered in my ear while he licked my lobe.

I giggled softly.

"Hum, I love when you take control like that, Steven."

He kissed my neck down to my shoulder, his teeth slightly scraping my skin.

"I know," he purred.

Deep in his chest, I could feel a deep rumble coming from his wolf, a purr of satisfaction. I stayed in his arms for a while, basking in this moment of perfection.

"I can't believe how much I love you," he whispered in my ear. "No words could ever express what I feel for you."

I smiled at his words. "I will always be yours," I whispered to him.

He whispered back, "As I am also yours."

I kissed his delicious lips, tasting him again, as I could never have enough of him.

Only when we decided to get out of the bath did I realize how much water had spilled on the ground.

"Oh, my gosh! We better wipe this off." I exclaimed.

Steven laughed. "You're so perfect to me, my love. Go rest on the bed. I'll clean this up."
I was glad to let Steven mop up the water. Although I felt more energized than earlier, I was still feeling tired.

As I waited for Steven to join me, a knock came at the door. I was still naked and wouldn't have time to get dressed. I knew the door was locked.

I shouted, "Yes?"

A throat cleared on the other side of the door. "Madam, the dinner will be served soon. The King and the Queen are waiting for you to join them in the dining hall."

I hadn't realized how much time had passed since we had arrived. I needed to get ready, and fast.

I answered, "Thank you! We will be joining shortly."

I waited for the servant to answer anything, but no sound was coming from the door, meaning he was probably gone.

Steven finally came out of the bathroom. "Steven! We need to get to the dining room!"
He smirked at me. "Are you planning to go like that?"
I laughed at his joke. "No, you dumbass! But we'd better prepare!"
He burst out laughing. He loved to make dumb jokes like this, and he knew I liked it too. He brushed a kiss on my lips and grabbed the dress he got while shopping this afternoon.
"Why don't you put this on? I'm sure you'll look amazing."

I looked at the powder blue dress. It sparkled under the light and I could definitely feel the magic coming from it. I was scared it would be too tight, but it fit perfectly. It looked like it was made especially for me. As I put it on, I instantly felt refreshed. I could feel the magic flowing through me. I didn't know what powers the dress held, but it was a blessing.
I tied my hair, freeing my shoulders, leaving some loose strands. I turned my head to Steven's whistle.
"Wow! You look even more amazing than I thought you'd be."
I grinned at Steven's comment. Then I looked him over, from head to toe. He had changed into formal black pants with a classic white shirt. The shirt was a little tight over his muscled chest, and I thought he looked sexy.

"You don't look too bad either, wolf." I winked at him.

I loved to tease him by calling him like that. His wolf purred softly at me.

"Why don't we get to the dining hall, before I devour you... And this time, I'll use my mouth," teased, Steven.

I sucked in a breath. "Well, when you put it like that, I'm not sure we should go."

He laughed at my statement and pulled me towards the door. "I think we'd better join the King and Queen."

He winked as I giggled. "Yes, I think you're right."

Chapter 9 (Blake)

Fiery Flower

I exited the throne room and went directly to the servants' quarters. My heart was beating fast. I was eager to see her. I still couldn't believe how much this woman affected me. Now that I had found my mate, I wouldn't let her go. I would find a way to make her see how perfect she was. I would take the time to discover how she felt about me. She seemed so shy. She had built a shell to protect herself from hurtful memories. I had managed to learn about the past of her race a little. I needed to remember to go read about that, or to convince her to tell me more about it. My heart sank when she said her family was killed when she was a child. That must have been so hard! No wonder she was hiding in her shell. I only hoped I would be able to get her out of it.

The kitchen was busy as ever when I entered. Everything smelled so delicious. Scalanis flinched when he saw me. Good. The way that bastard was talking to her earlier, I wouldn't hesitate to put my threat to execution. All my anger disappeared when I saw her. She was wearing an apron on top of her black pants. She wore a white blouse on top. She didn't need any jewelry to be gorgeous. I walked up to her, Scalanis stepping out of my way as I advanced into the kitchen.

She was cooking brown sauce in a pot. I stood behind her. I wasn't sure what to say. I didn't want to startle her. Just as I was about to say something, she turned around. She shrieked and dropped her wooden spatula when she saw me. I refrained from laughing, but couldn't hide my smile. She put a hand on her chest, then smiled when she realized it was me.

"Don't scare me like that!"

I chuckled as she picked up the fallen spatula.

"Sorry, I didn't mean to. I was trying to say something, but you turned before I could."

She glanced nervously behind me, looking at Scalanis. A growl escaped my chest. That man needed to stay down.

"What are you doing here?" she whispered.

"I needed to tell you," I told her happily. "I'll be able to taste your food. I'll be eating dinner with the King and Queen tonight."

She blushed at my statement.

"Oh, really?" She seemed lost in her thoughts.

"Hey, don't worry. I'm sure it'll taste as good as you."

Her eyes went wide. That's when I realized what I had just said.

"What?"

I rubbed the back of my head. "I… it's not what I meant. Sorry," I told her apologetically. "I meant that I'm sure you make amazing food."

Her smile looked like the most precious treasure I could lay my eyes on. When she smiled, the yellow jewel embedded in her chest glowed. I wondered what it was. I guess I'd have to ask her, eventually.

I snarled when Scalanis cleared his throat from behind me.

Eshenesra whispered, "You can't stay here. We need to prepare the rest of the banquet."

I nodded. "Okay, I'll see you later, then."

I stared at Scalanis as I exited the kitchen. He didn't dare say anything to me.

I got to my room and changed into formal black pants. It's not every day that you got to eat at the same table as a King and a Queen. I didn't own a formal shirt, so the butler let me borrow one from the royal wardrobe. I found a deep blue one that fit me well. I tied my hair neatly. I was surprised when I looked in the mirror. I smirked at my reflection; I didn't know I could look that good.

The supper was held at the banquet hall. It was a very long room. Stained glass windows let the light from the sun enter the room, and chandeliers brightened up the room even more. The walls were made of stone. On one side was a big fireplace, heating up the room. There was a small stage near the fireplace. A bard was playing the guitar and signing a song about some adventurers.

"Heareth the st'ry of Tanur, and its spice trad'rs! F'r admiral Cilistinu, Valentina, Vernu the myst'rious royal chef, and royal weapons exp'rt Alessandro, shall saileth the flotes, visiteth exotic islands, battleth legendary beasts, and consume most wondrous food."

Beside the stage was a dancing floor. It was empty for now, but it would surely fill up after supper. There were five long tables lined up together to form one very long table. Light blue tablecloths with gold threads of embroidery were covering the tables. Candles, food plates, and centerpieces were aligned on the tables. The king and the queen were sitting at one end of the table. I was lucky to be sitting by their side, along with Steven and Bianca. We were the guests of honor.

Bianca and Steven were already there when I arrived. Bianca was wearing a dazzling dress. I think it was the dress Zach and Steven got for her when they went shopping. I was happy when Zach handed me leather wrist armor. It was reinforced and enchanted to give me a greater attack speed. I couldn't wait to see how it would feel in a battle.

The bard suddenly stopped singing, stood up, took a deep breath and shouted, *"Ev'ryone taketh a seat, the supp'r shall beest s'rved!"*

I was amazed at the sheer size of the bard! He was at least three heads taller than everyone! I wondered if he was from another part of the country to be talking like that. He did have elven ears, but his frame was thicker than elves.

"Everyone's impressed the first time they see him."

I turned around to see the king smiling at me. "And here I thought I was tall!" I exclaimed.

Alluin smiled at my remark. "His name is Adren. He is a firbolg."

"A firbolg?"

"Yes, from the giant race."

The giant race? I had heard legends about them. "I thought they lived very far away."

"They usually do. But this one met an elven woman a few years ago. They fell in love. He decided to live in the city with his wife. He's been the castle's bard ever since, while his wife takes care of their children."

I watched Adren. You could see how much he loved music the way he handled his instruments. Other musicians joined him on the stage, and they started playing a soft melody, while servants brought plates to the table.

There she was, my sweet Eshenesra. Even with her servant's apron, I thought she was prettier than a queen wearing the most precious dress. I could sense her heart beating faster as she got closer to me. She brushed against me as she placed my plate in front of me. That contact got me yearning for more.

I smiled at her. "Thank you."

She blushed and continued with her tasks. It was a shame I couldn't eat in her company. Nonetheless, I ate supper while talking with the King, the Queen, Steven, and Bianca. The food was delicious. Everyone was having a good time. A little further I recognized Iain, the guild's high mage. He was sitting at a table with a beautiful young elf. He seemed to enjoy her company quite a lot. She seemed to be having a good time, too.

After supper, people started to dance to the bard's music. Bianca and Steven kept talking with the King and the Queen. I thought of Zach, Arius, and Elashor. They've been gone for a few hours now. I wondered if they were already at Nokorath Hills. Would they be alright? Why was Will going there? What the hell was that creature he was flying on? Somehow, I had a bad feeling about this. I only hoped they would get some sense into him and get him back here safely.

My worries were forgotten when I saw Eshenesra standing alone in a corner of the room. Her fiery hair contrasted with her white servant's shirt. I couldn't see the jewel on her chest with this outfit, but I wondered if it was glowing, like earlier. She was staring at the floor. She didn't even notice me when I arrived by her side. The bard and the musicians were playing lively lounge music and people were dancing.

"Would you give me this dance?"

She was startled by the sound of my voice. "Blake!" She smiled. I offered her my arm.

"But… I don't even have a dress. I'm in my apron." I sucked in a breath. Surely, she didn't understand the effect she had on me.

"Eshenesra, you are the finest, loveliest, tenderest, and most beautiful person I have ever known… And even that is an understatement."

She was speechless. She stared at me, not knowing what to say, a single tear running down her cheek. "It would be an honor if you accepted to dance with me."
She stared at me with her golden eyes, setting fire to my soul. My heart skipped a beat when she nodded and grabbed my arm.

We danced to the song, our bodies moving in sync. Her hair was flowing as I twirled her; a fiery flower with a magnetic pull. She was luring me in, catching my soul in her flaming eyes. I was sure every woman tonight wished they dazzled and shined as bright as she did.

I kept her close to me, yearning for her skin and her touch. I was craving her. My vampiric instincts were getting pushy. The scent of her skin was intoxicating me. I fought my instincts down. The fact we were in a room surrounded by people helped greatly.
After a few songs, she suddenly stopped dancing. She whispered, "I'm sorry, Blake."
"What is it?"

I didn't understand why she was apologizing so suddenly.

"I need to get going."

My heart sank at those words.

"Please, stay a little longer."

Her eyes were sad, and her voice was shaky as she answered, "I can't."

I tried to keep her hand in mine, but it slipped away. I didn't even have the time to tell her how I felt, or to try to kiss her. She was gone so fast; I didn't see where she went. Around me, the music was still playing, and people were still dancing.

I didn't understand what was happening. Did I do something wrong? I would need to ask her when I see her next.

I got back to the table, where Iain was now talking with the king. I glanced around the room to see Bianca and Steven dancing. I drank my cup of blood wine, still wondering what's got Eshenesra to leave in such a hurry.

"Are you enjoying yourself?" a melodious voice got me out of my thought.

I smiled at Solandra.

"Yes, my queen."

"You seemed lost in your thoughts."

I nodded to her. "I suppose I was."

"Would you mind giving me the next dance?" she asked me.

I was surprised by her request.

"Will the King be okay with me dancing with you?"

She smiled. "I'm afraid my husband is very busy with his lively conversations with your friend. I am accustomed to dancing with the nobles during our banquets, but it seems that none of them have asked me tonight."

Surely, I couldn't say no to the queen. As long as the king wouldn't mind, then I could spare a dance.

I made a small neck bow. "It would be my pleasure."

The queen grabbed my arm, and we walked to the center of the dance floor. People crowded to the sides, making room for us, and the musicians began to play a waltz. Fortunately, I knew how to dance, having learned it hundreds of years before. The queen danced graciously, her body almost gliding through the air as I led the waltz. Dancing with the queen was nice, and she smelled like a delicate flower. But this was pure politesse. After the music stopped, she did a small curtsey, and I bowed, and we went our different ways. The music started again, and people filled the dance floor.

There was no point in my staying here. Eshenesra was long gone. We had a big day ahead of us tomorrow. I decided to retire to my room.

As I made my way through the deserted corridors, I heard someone's cries. I followed the sound. It got louder as I got closer. My chest tightened as a draft of Eshenesra's scent caught my nose. I walked faster, still following the sound of crying. It led to a small room. The door was slightly open. My heart stopped when my fear was confirmed; This was Eshenesra's room. I could see her sitting on her bed, crying. I couldn't help myself and entered the room.

My body was aching. I couldn't hold in the tears that were flowing onto my cheeks. He was so angry at me. Nothing could stop him.
I lifted my head to the sound of someone walking, scared that he was back. He wasn't. It was Blake. Warmth filled my heart at his sight, but also shame. I didn't want him to see me like this. What would he think of me?

I pulled my shawl over my shoulders.
He asked with a soft voice, "What's going on?"
The thoughts of Scalanis hitting me again and again filled me. Even after I begged him to stop. All I could think of was protecting my eyes with my hands. The pain, leaving bruises on my body, until I felt numb. I had no idea what I had done to make him this angry. He looked like his eyes would pop out of his head. I had never seen such fury. He kept asking me, "Why? You fucking whore!" But I had no idea what he meant. At least usually he was careful not to leave a mark. This time, he lashed out everything he had.
I watched Blake's dark eyes. He was waiting for an answer. I wouldn't dare to tell him what happened. I felt so ashamed.
People walked into the hallway, glancing inside the room.
Blake frowned.
"This room isn't good enough for you. Everyone can see and hear everything. Come to my room, you'll be better."

He offered me his hand. Was he really inviting me to his room? He had one of the nicest guest rooms in the castle. The only time I was allowed in a room like that was to clean it up.

His voice was gentle.

"Will you come with me?"

I couldn't believe how nice he was with me. He was the opposite of Scalanis.

My heart was pounding when he was close. Yet, I feared being hurt if I let myself fall for him.

I grabbed his hand and followed him through the halls to his room. The pain of each step reminded me that my body was probably bruised in many places. Luckily, the shawl over my shoulders hid my arms, hiding them from Blake.

Blake was walking slowly, following my pace, leading me gently towards his room.

I was amazed by Blake's room. It was so nice! I dreamt of the day I'd be able to have such a beautiful room with a big, comfortable bed. My servant's room was so small compared to this one. The room even had a complete bathroom attached to it. I would feel like a princess if I had such a room.

Life was so cruel. To have been born a dark elf, despised by the other races. I only hoped one day to be able to live a normal life, on my own, in the city. I didn't want to resort to the underground market, like so many other dark elves did. Performing the disgusting tasks that other races gave. The worst jobs that no one else wanted to do. Poisoning people, killing innocents, kidnapping children, stealing family jewels… The list went on. Working at the castle was at least a dignifying work, despite what Scalanis was making me go through.

Blake's voice was gentle. "Why were you crying?"

I could never tell him the truth. I didn't know what he would do if I would. I feared his re-action.

"I was yelled after, because I danced with you."

I didn't understand why Scalanis was so an-gry, but at least I understood it was related to the fact that I danced with Blake. I gasped as a menac-ing growl escaped Blake's chest. I could see anger in his eyes. I got back a few inches, scared of what he could do. Seeing my reaction, Blake's face re-laxed.

"I'm sorry. I didn't mean to scare you. I would never hurt you."

I let out a breath at those words, my heart-beat returning to normal.

"I don't understand why someone would yell at you for dancing with me. I'm so sorry. I wouldn't want anyone being mean to you because of me."

He grabbed my hands and pulled me gently closer to him. Despite him being gentle, I cried softly from the pain in my arms. My shawl fell from my shoulders onto the bed, revealing my bruised arms. Blake's eyes widened at the sight of my bruised body. I tried to put the shawl back, but he stopped me. He softly brushed his fingers over my bruises.

His eyes were burning with anger, but his voice was soft.

"Who did this to you?"

I swallowed hard. I knew he wouldn't let this go now that he had seen the bruises. I had no choice but to tell him. I took a deep breath before answering.

"Scalanis."

He gritted his teeth hard.

"Why did he hurt you?"

I whispered, my words barely escaping my lips, "I'm not sure. I think it's because I danced with you."

Blake clenched his fists hard, a low, menacing growl escaping from his chest.

"I will hurt anyone who hurts you. It's about time I taught this motherfucker a lesson."

I was downright frightened of what could happen if he were to go see Scalanis. Panic filled me at this thought.

I screamed with a small voice, "Please don't!"

He barked, "Are you protecting him now?"

I recoiled at the tone of his voice, shrinking back a little, and shook my head. "I'm scared he'll get back at me afterwards, if you go to see him."

All the anger disappeared from Blake. His burning eyes were now filled with sadness. I sat on the bed, exhaustion washing over me from all the conflicting emotions.

I added with a small voice, "I don't understand why you would do this for me."

Blake got down on the bed, grabbing my hands in his.

"Didn't you hear what I told you earlier? You are the most delicate, yet fiery flower I could ever wish for. Never in my life have I felt something similar for any woman. You light a fire deep within my soul. I have no words to describe how strongly I fell for you in such a short amount of time!"

His words were too good to be true. My heart felt like it was beating so fast, it would get out of my chest. I knew he was sincere. I couldn't keep going on like this. I felt the same.

I pressed my lips onto his, sparks igniting inside of me. The fire of my lips met with the coldness of his. My birthmark glowed strongly as we kissed. My heart fluttered as I tasted him for the first time. He grabbed my thighs and brought me closer, so that I was straddling on him.

I was amazed at how gentle those strong arms could be. His fingers were running down my back, sending me shivers. For the first time in my life, I felt like I was precious.

We broke the kiss. It was already late, and I needed to get up early to do the tasks in the castle. "As much as I would like to stay, I need to get to bed. I wake up early in the morning to do my tasks."

Blake let me go, reluctantly. He picked up my shawl and gave it back. I picked it up, still shaking from being beaten up.

Blake asked in a deep, soft tone, "Would you stay with me? For the night?"

My eyes opened wide. Was he asking what I thought he was?

He added quickly, "I just want to be with you. Nothing more. Just to know you're safe."

I smiled. This seemed like a nice thought. "Okay."

Blake smiled at my answer and grabbed me in his strong arms as if I was the most precious woman in the world.

He whispered, "You have no idea how happy you've just made me."

We laid under the covers. Blake wrapped me in his arms. It felt so good! I inhaled his manly scent and laid my head on his chest. My birthmark glowed brightly.

"Can I ask you? What is this on your chest?"

"It's a birthmark. I have no idea what it's for."

Blake touched it with the tip of his finger, making it twinkle.

"It's beautiful. It looks like a jewel."

I had never thought of it this way. "Thank you."

"Is it always glowing like that?"

I shook my head. "Only when I'm with you."

Blake smiled before adding, "Then it must mean something special."

I smiled. "That must be true."

Fatigue was overwhelming me, making me yawn.

"I guess I should let you sleep."

I giggled. "That sounds like a good idea."

He gently grabbed the back of my head, bringing my lips to his, kissing me softly while playing with my hair. I knew I would sleep tight. No nightmares would visit me tonight.

Chapter 10 (Will)

The Downfall

I held her by the neck. I could hear her struggle to breathe as I squeezed tighter. Her chest rose more rapidly as her lungs tried to get the air it desperately needed. Her eyes now had a red taint to them as they filled with blood. Her once white skin was now turning blue. Her white hair that was once flowing with the wind, now rested lifeless on her back. She was strong and gave a good fight. But nothing would get in the way of me resurrecting my mate. Her hands were losing their grip on my arm, her eyes rolling inside their orbits.

"Good job," encouraged the demon.

My eyes sparkled with excitement as I knew that soon I would have the power needed to resurrect my sweet Leila.

She was numb, her body was heavy, barely alive. I could have easily taken the Desire's Etcher, wedged between her breasts. But I wanted to feel her soul leave her body.

Not that she could send her guards to take it back from me. The air nymphs' bodies laid on the

174

ground, across daggers and swords. They were merely bugs for me to crush. The storm that was raging on top of the mountain had died when I started killing them. As if growing weaker with each soul I claimed. Eurynomos kept guiding me, instructing me of what I needed to do in order to get my mate back. He seemed pleased with my progress.

"What the hell are you doing?" shouted a voice behind me.

I once knew that voice. It belonged to someone who was once important to me. It seemed like such a long time ago. Now, however, all that mattered was getting my mate back.

I turned around to see Zach, Arius, and an elven woman. They were looking around them, horrified. The elven woman held a hand in front of her mouth, gagging at the sight of so many corpses.

I answered nonchalantly, "What does it look like? Killing her."

"Why are you doing this?" asked Zach.

I raised a brow. "Why not?"

They looked at me with disgusted looks on their faces.

"What happened to you? You're different."

I stared at them. What did they mean? Yes, I had accepted powers from the demon, but it was only so that I could resurrect my mate. Anyone would have done the same. It didn't change who I was.

Seeing I wasn't answering anything, Zach added, "Look at yourself in a mirror, Will."

I walked to the iced lake, still holding the nymph's neck in my hand. I watched my reflection on the ice. Black veins were spreading across my face. As I studied my reflection, I realized the Nymph's Queen was not living anymore. I dislodged the precious dagger from her breasts, then tossed the corpse away.

I turned back to Zach and the others and shrugged my shoulders.

"I don't know, and I don't care. I need to get back to Leila."

Zach took a step back.

"Will, she's dead."

"She's not!" I growled in rage, the ice around us cracking from the power of my shout.

A piece of ice separated itself from the mountain and fell down a few yards away. The elven woman got closer to Arius.

My words rang with the power of my determination as I spoke.

"I will bring her back."

"It's impossible," answered Zach.

"Nothing is impossible to me anymore," I gritted through my teeth.

I rejoiced at the fear I could read in their eyes. They should know to fear me if they were to try to stop me.

Zach asked, "Did you… gain power somehow?"

I snarled at him, "What if I did?"

"What… are you?" asked Zach.

"What do you think?" Laughed Eurynomos before adding, *"What are you going to do about it, you ignorant fool?"* spat Eurynomos from inside me, making my voice sound lower than it normally was.

I shouted out loud at Eurynomos, "Shut the fuck up, demon! You can't speak if I don't decide that you're allowed to!" That demon needed to know his place.

Realizing what had happened, Zach asked. "How could you? You sided with the one who killed your mate! He's foul! He can't be trusted."

I gestured with my arm, a wave of power blowing the snow in front of them.
"Shut up! He has the strength I need to revive Leila. You can't understand what it feels like to lose your mate, the one made for you."

They stopped talking. Arius took a step closer.
"I do."
I watched the vampire Prince. It was true. He had known what it felt like to lose his mate. But then, he was here today with an elven woman.
"It's true, your mate was killed. So, I guess you found yourself a whore to bide your time until you join her again in the afterlife."
Arius pulled the elven woman into his arm.
"Don't you dare mix Elashor into this. Fate has given me a second chance at love."

I spat at them. "Fate doesn't give second chances."

Arius screamed at me, shielding Elashor with his body.

"Will, I know it hurts. I've been there before. But it's not too late. Come with us. Let the demon alone. What would Leila think of this?"

I turned my head away from them. "It's too late for me."

I started to make my way back to the gargoyle, when I heard Zach's voice, "We won't let you."

Rage boiled inside of me, making the ground rumble. They wanted to stop me. They could try. I wouldn't let them.

Zach and Arius jumped on me, launching punches at me, but I was way too fast for them. I dodged every attack they gave. Elashor was shooting arrows at me, but I was moving too fast for her. Sincerely, I pitied how weak they were.
Was I once so weak?

Zach was stronger than Arius, but still, it wasn't enough. He tried to kick at my face, but I moved so fast that I was behind his back, punching him in the face as he turned to look at me, surprised. Blood gushed out of his broken nose. But still, he kept coming back.

Arius tried to slash me with his sharp nails. I kicked him in the chest so hard that he fell a few feet in the air and smashed into a rock with a loud crack. The rock shattered from the impact and his body hit the floor. I wondered how many bones had broken in that hit. Hopefully, enough to keep him down. What annoying bastards. Elashor ran to him in panic.

Zach picked up a sword that was lying on the ground. He slashed towards me, trying to get it in my gut. I jumped in the air and dodged the blade, landing a kick to his face at the same time.

"You want to play with weapons?" I snarled at him.
I focused on the ground. Two tekpis tore from one of the corpses to my hands, blood still dripping. "Let's play," I taunted him.

Zach kept swinging his sword at me, or even trying to slash me with his nails, but I was way too fast for him. So sad that this powerful werewolf-vampire was so useless. Were these the best hope against the power of the demon? This world was doomed from the beginning. Leila shouldn't have sacrificed herself for this…
"How pathetic, indeed," agreed the demon inside of me.

Countless times, I slashed his arm with the tekpi, his blood tainting the ground. He swung his sword at me and hit my arm. I pushed him back with a kick to the chest. Zach cried in pain as bones in his rib cage broke.

At the same time, Arius got back up, hold-ing his rib cage. Despite the pain, he tried to launch an attack with his vampiric powers on me. My hair swayed with the wind from his attack. I didn't feel anything from his attack. I had enough of this. It was time for me to end this.

I moved swiftly and got to Elashor without them noticing. She screamed as I carried the tekpi pointing to her neck.

I shouted at them, holding her in place,

"Are you done playing yet?"

She was trying to break free from my hold, but I was way stronger than her.

"Don't you fucking dare," threatened Arius. Zach's wolf was growling at me.

"I'm done dealing with you, annoying fools. Don't you see? You've lost already," I shouted to them with disdain. "I have more pressing matters to attend to, anyway."

I stabbed into Elashor's shoulder before pushing her to the floor. She shrieked in pain as Arius and Zach ran to her.

I made my way to the gargoyle that was waiting for me.

"Will! We're not done yet!" screamed Zach.

I dismissed them with my hand. "I'm done."

I got onto the back of the gargoyle and took flight. I had to get back to the castle. I had the enchanted dagger. It was time I revived my sweet Leila.

*********** Blake's POV ************

I woke up still holding Eshenesra in my arms. She was my black diamond, my fiery flower. Her heavenly lilac scent was intoxicating me. It took me forever to fall asleep last night. I craved for her so much. All I could think of was how much I wanted to claim her, to make her mine. How I wanted to sink my teeth into her neck. I wanted to become one with her. But she was wounded, and she needed to rest.

My eyes fell on her bruises again. I was so mad at Scalanis. The only thing that was preventing me from confronting him was that I didn't want him to unleash his rage upon her. I wanted to protect her, to keep her by my side. It was clear to me that there was no way I was leaving this city without her. I would find a way to get her to come with me.

After sleeping with her in my arms, I knew I didn't want to sleep without her again. It was scary. All my life, I had only myself to care about. I never had to worry. I could fight with all that I had. The worst that could ever happen was for me to die. But today, everything changed. For the first time, I was scared of losing someone dear to me. And it scared the hell out of me. I would give my life to protect her. I would kill whoever hurts her. I would do everything I could to make her smile as often as possible. I wanted her to feel safe with me. I wanted her to open up to me. I wanted her to know that she could share her deepest secrets with me.

She began stirring in her sleep, opening her eyes, gracing me with her golden stare.
"Hey there, beautiful."

She smiled. "I'm so glad this wasn't a dream."

I laughed low and kissed her. "You bet; it wasn't a dream!"

She asked lazily, "What time is it?" I didn't get to answer before she freaked out. "I'm probably late for work!"

I tried to make her relax. "Calm down! I'll take the blame."

She stared into my eyes. "Do you think it will work?"

I grinned. "I'll make it work."

I changed in the bathroom. Eshenesra didn't have a change of clothes with her, so she waited for me.

We got down to get our breakfast. As we ate, Scalanis entered the room, screaming.

"Eshenesra! There you are! Where have you been? You good-for-nothing wench!"

I gritted my teeth. It took all that I had not to jump on him and drink his life away. I gave him a stern look. I couldn't hurt him in front of the King and Queen. But I could use my powers without anyone knowing.

I smirked at this thought and pushed my vampiric dark force towards him. He suddenly stopped moving and stared at me, his pulse rising from fear. I sneered; he could feel it alright.

The queen was walking by on the other side of the room. She wasn't feeling my powers as I directed them at Scalanis only.

She raised a brow and asked Scalanis, "Is something the matter?"

I didn't let him answer anything. He tried to speak, but I stole his voice away. His eyes opened wide as he continued to open his mouth to speak, but not a sound came out of it.

I turned towards the Queen and spoke apologetically.

"I'm sorry, your Majesty. I have kept Eshenesra busy this morning, and thus, she is late for her tasks."

The queen nodded. "I'm sure Scalanis was able to get everything done by someone else." She turned her head towards him. "Weren't you?"
Scalanis was still frozen in place by my powers. He simply nodded, his mouth open, sweat beading on his forehead.

I added, "With all due respect, your Majesty. I think Miss Eshenesra is not feeling well today. Would it be possible for her to take a day to rest?"

Solandra nodded and smiled. "Well, of course! That shouldn't be a problem, right Scalanis?"

Slowly, he shook his head.

Happy with how things were going, I released my powers.

Scalanis took a breath, as if emerging from the depths of the waters, seeming to catch his breath. He glanced at me and Eshenesra, but didn't dare say anything. I hoped this scared him enough that he would stay away from Eshenesra. He bowed to the queen and left the room.

Bianca and Steven entered the room and started eating their breakfast. Eshenesra seemed more relaxed now that she could have the day off. She still had her shawl over her shoulders. I wondered how long it would take for her wounds to heal.

"My goodness!" screamed, Bianca.
I looked up towards the door to see Zach, Arius, and Elashor walking inside the room. They were wounded, bleeding on the floor, and limping. Elashor had a weapon lodged in her shoulder.

I shouted to them, "What happened to you?"
Arius answered in a hoarse voice, "Will did this."
Bianca put a hand over her mouth. She whispered, "That can't be!"
Zach took a seat at the table, wincing with pain as he did. Arius continued talking while holding Elashor by the waist.
"Will… he's changed. He has sided with Eurynomos."

I was baffled. I couldn't believe what Arius just said. This was impossible. Eurynomos was responsible for Leila's death. Will couldn't possibly side with his mate's murderer.
I answered, "I don't believe it!"
Zach replied, "It's true… Somehow, he thinks he can revive Leila."
Bianca shouted, "But that can't be! I don't believe you!"

Elashor answered in a soft voice, "Yet, somehow it's true."

Bianca replied, "We need to stop him."
It was unbelievable. I couldn't believe that Will had joined the demon's side. Especially after what happened to his mate.
I asked them, "Do you have any idea where he is?"
Arius answered, "He was flying north on his creature. He must have a base or something over there."

Bianca answered, "I'm not ready to go there yet. I still need to train."
I replied, "That's true. We should go to the magic guild. Maybe we could get a healing spell done on you three at the same time."
They all looked at me and nodded.

Bianca added, "That's an excellent idea. We'll leave tomorrow morning to fight Will."
Zach replied, "But we don't know where Will is."
Bianca answered, "We don't know… yet. We have all day to figure this out."
Steven replied, "I'll go around town and ask."
Elashor answered, "I need to get that thing out of my shoulder… But I'll help afterwards."
Eshenesra added, "I don't know what this is all about, but I'll help as well."
My heart warmed at those words and I murmured to her, "I would love to have you come with us."

I was shocked to see the state they were in. The elven woman even had a weapon lodged into her shoulder. I wasn't sure I understood everything that was going on here, but I knew I wanted to help them. I followed them to the city since Blake had talked the Queen into giving me a day off. Which I was feeling so grateful for.

I stayed close to him as we walked in the streets. We quickly got to the magic guild. Bianca turned towards us.

"I'll get Iain to spare a healing potion for you guys," she said, pointing to the wounded ones. Then she added, "Elashor, please come with me. We'll remove this tekpi from your shoulder."

The elven woman followed her inside. We waited outside for a while; Blake was talking with Zach.

"This is bad. I can't believe Will decided to side with Eurynomos."

"He's so powerful! I was barely able to scratch him."

"I only hope that Bianca's powers will be strong enough for her to fight him off."

"There's got to be something we can use to help us."

This was serious. I wasn't sure if it was a good idea, but I proposed, "Maybe you could use some poison?"

They both looked at me. I waited anxiously for a reaction from them.

"That could be a good idea," said Blake.

"Do you know where we could get some?" asked Zach.

I nodded to them. "I could lead you to the underground market."

Blake's eyes widened. "You know how to gain entrance to it?"

"Yes… Most of the dark elves work there. I try to avoid it, but I know where it is."

"Then it's settled!" said Zach. "We will head there."

"Not before you drink this," stated Bianca, handing him a flask.

At her side was Elashor, who seemed all healed. Zach drank the potion while Bianca gave one to Arius.

"Where are you guys heading?" asked Bianca.

"We're going to the underground market to get some poison to use against Will," stated Zach.

Bianca put a hand on her mouth. Zach put a hand on her shoulder. "Bianca, I know Will is your brother. But he's sided with the demon, and he's stronger than ever. We need everything we can to help us defeat him." He sighed, then added, "Don't forget he's also my nephew."

The word seemed to weigh a lot on his shoulders.

"Well, I think I should go and see that knick-knack shop," said Elashor.

"You mean Kõrvits?" asked Arius.

Elashor grinned and got a small pocket watch out. "Yes, I'm sure he has all kinds of useful gizmos we can use to fight. Didn't he say he used to build robots to fight for him?"

"That's an excellent idea!" exclaimed Bianca. "You guys do that while I train further."

"Perfect, I'll go to the underground market with Eshenesra," stated Zach.

"So will I," added Blake. My heart fluttered at the fact that Blake was coming as well.

"Then I'll go with Arius and Elashor to the knick-knack shop," said Steven.

"It's called 'Ye Olde Atelier,'" added Elashor.

"Alright, have some fun you guys," said Bianca before kissing Steven goodbye.

"Say 'hi' to Kõrvits for me," added Blake with a smile.

This shop sure sounded fun. It sounded more fun than going to the underground market. As we prepared to go, Blake squeezed my hand and whispered to me, "Thanks for helping me."
Those words alone made my heart flutter. Keeping away from him was proving impossible. I dreaded the day he would leave. For now, I was happy to spend the day with him.

I walked through the streets with Zach and Blake. It was weird to be the one leading the way. I was used to following orders and following others.

Not the other way around. But it was refreshing as well.

Soon, we arrived at a dark street. There had been a major fire a few years ago. The houses and shops burned, but people didn't deem it worth being rebuilt. Wooden planks blocked the windows. Some houses didn't have doors anymore. Some people still lived in those ruins; rejected, unwanted, unwelcome. The scum of all races, living amongst themselves, the only place that wouldn't scream at their sight. Some of them were spying on us as we hastily made our way through the street.
"Ignore them," I whispered to Zach and Blake before increasing the pace.

We soon arrived at what was once a guard's tower. It was spared by the fire; its walls being made of rocks and the door being made of metal. The guards had long abandoned it. There was no need to protect the people living in the slums.

I knocked three times on the metal door. The heavy metal door creaked open just enough to let a man examine us from inside.
He asked warily, "What do you want?"
I whispered, "We come for the goods."
The man grunted, "We don't have goods here."
I spat back at him, "I know damn well you have goods! Now stop playing dumb and let us in. I know Darren."

The man's eyes widened. Darren was well known in the underground market. Nothing more needed to be said. He opened the door and let us in.

The room was dark, lit up by candles along the wall.

I gestured to Blake and Zach. "Follow me."

I followed the corridor until we arrived at a big open room. Beyond it was another big open room, and then another. These were ancient barracks and training grounds for the guards that had been converted into a big marketplace. Tables lined up against the wall and at the center of the rooms. You could barely walk between the stalls.
Customers were browsing the goods, keeping to themselves. No one really wanted to be seen in the underground market. Sellers often kept hoods on. Others didn't care, as their faces were plastered on wanted posters.

I walked with Zach and Blake, letting them browse through the goods. Blake kept holding my hand.

Soon, I spotted what I was looking for.
"Darren!" I exclaimed with pleasure.
The dark elf smiled at me; his green eyes glowing when he saw me.
"Eshenesra! It's been a long time! And you brought friends as well."
I smiled back at him.
"This is Zach and Blake. They are fighting against a demon, from what I understand."
"A demon!" Darren's voice was filled with astonishment as he spoke.

"Nice to meet you," said Blake in a deep voice.

"A very powerful demon," added Zach.

"I thought you might have something that could help them defeat it," I said to Darren.

He grinned at my statement.

"Of course! Now, let me check," he answered, while searching through his vials.

Zach added, "We might not get a lot of chances to hit him. Something strong would probably be the best."

Blake stared at him. "What if it kills him?"

"Believe me. I've seen his strength. Poison won't kill him."

"Ah!" Exclaimed Darren, having found what he was looking for. He held a small black vial in his hand.

"This is the most potent poison that I have. It's believed to come from the Gorgons directly! Of course, one can never be sure of where these come from. It's very rare!"

Zach said, pondering, "The Gorgons! Now that's interesting. We'll take it."

Darren smiled. "That will be five thousand pieces."

I shouted, "Five thousand pieces?! That's more pieces than what I earn in a year!"

Zach picked a pouch from his belt, counted some pieces, and gave them to Darren.

"There you go!" he said, as he picked up the vial given by Darren.

"Where the hell did you get this money?"
Blake asked.

Zach grinned. "The vampire Lord wanted
to make sure we had everything we needed on our
journey."

Darren told them, "Just open the vial and
pour the content on the blade of your sword when
you fight."

I thanked him dearly. "Anytime, my
friend."

He waved as we left his stall.

We made our way back to the exit, while
Blake and Zach still fought over the price paid for
the poison's vial. It was funny to watch them. They
looked like two brothers arguing.

We slowly made our way back to the castle.
I had the day off, so I guess I could relax in my
quarters. Maybe enjoy some time outside in the gar-
dens.

As we arrived at the castle, Blake stopped
talking. He was serious. I was wondering what was
going on, but I didn't dare to ask.
"Thanks for showing us the underground market,"
said Zach.

I nodded to him. For the first time in my
life, I really felt like I had friends with me. People
who cared about me, and whom I could rely on. I
was afraid of losing them. I hoped I would be able
to keep them in my life as long as possible.

"I was happy to be with you guys," I said
heartily.

Blake looked at me. "I will see you later. Please enjoy your day off."

I nodded to him and watched worriedly as he entered the castle and went directly to the throne's room. He didn't even kiss me goodbye. He barely said anything and looked in a hurry to go speak with the King. I wondered why.

Chapter 11 (Bianca)

Consumed

I still couldn't believe Will had teamed up with the demon that killed his mate. This just didn't make any sense. My brother… I loved him so much. I was determined now more than ever to master my powers. I would get some sense into him. I would save my brother.

My legs were trembling, but I kept pushing on. The thought of Will kept me fighting beyond my limits. I needed to be strong, to be there for my big brother. I would defeat Eurynomos and get my brother back. We will get through this together, as we should.

"Bianca, take a break! That's enough for now."

I panted and nodded to Iain. I had trained all morning and all afternoon. I had mastered the basics. I was now learning to harvest the Moon Goddess's powers. It was putting such a strain on my body, but I knew I was strong enough to do it.

Iain stared at me. "That dress you're wearing. It's magic, isn't?"

I nodded. "That's what I was told. When I put it on the other day, I immediately felt refreshed and could feel magic flowing through my veins."

Iain was thoughtful for a moment. "If I was to guess, I'd say it probably regenerates your health and mana. It's a very powerful dress."

Regeneration? I didn't know this was possible! It could explain why I was able to train so fiercely without collapsing.

"That's very useful!" I thought out loud.

"Shall we eat lunch before continuing?"

I nodded to him. The magic guild clerk brought us tuna sandwiches.

After lunch, we spent the afternoon training more. By the end of the day, I felt like I finally learned how to control this magic that was flowing through my veins. I was able to bend it to my will. Attacking fiercely, protecting, or healing myself. I felt like the dress helped greatly, as I never seemed to run out of mana either. It was a good thing. We were supposed to leave tomorrow to stop Will.

The clerk came to fetch us while we were taking a short break.

"I'm sorry to interrupt. Her lady's friends are here."

"Already?" I asked, surprised.

I looked at the clock to see it was already late afternoon.

Iain spoke with a sincere smile, "I think you're ready, my dear."

I turned my head in surprise towards Iain.

"You think so?"

He nodded to me. I couldn't help but to hug him. "Oh, thank you for your help, Iain!"

"It was nothing," he answered, winking. "Now then, be careful and go save the world."

I got down the stairs to be greeted by Arius, Elashor, and my sweet Steven. My heart fluttered at his sight.

I pushed through to his mind. "How I've missed you!"

I heard his wolf purr before he answered, "I missed you too, my love."

"How was the training?" asked Elashor.

I grinned. "It was great! Iain says he thinks I'm ready."

"Perfect!" answered Elashor.

We started to walk towards the castle. I noticed that Arius was carrying a big, heavy box.

"What's that?" I asked.

Arius answered, "That's a little something Kõrvits gave us. It's his way of helping with the fight."

"Stop making me wait! I want to know what it is."

He laughed. "You'll see when we're back at the castle. I want Blake and Zach to see it, too."

I sighed, frustrated. "Fine, okay, let's get back already, then."

*********** Will's POV ************

As I flew back to the castle on the gargoyle, I couldn't help but to rejoice. At last, I had the Desire's Etcher. It was time to revive my sweet Leila. I couldn't wait to hold her in my arms again. As I flew near the castle, I noticed some of the battalion was outside, guarding the castle. Good. They had better protect the castle and Leila.

The gargoyle landed on the roof of the castle. I entered by the attic and got down.
I caught a glimpse of my reflection as I walked in front of a mirror. I stopped for a minute, staring at my reflection. My skin was strewn with black patches. The blue of my eyes had darkened to the point you could barely make the difference between the iris and the pupil. I grunted. This wasn't good. At this rate, Leila wouldn't recognize me when she lives again.

I yelled at Eurynomos, "You didn't warn me about this, demon!"
A growl escaped my chest, but it wasn't coming from my wolf, it was coming from the demon. I realized it had been a while since I had spoken with my wolf and wondered if he was still suffering from the severing of the mate bond.

Annoyed, Eurynomos answered, *"Relax, wolf boy. She will recognize you through your mate bond."*
I let out a breath of relief. It's true, I hadn't thought about the mate bond. Of course, she would recognize me. She couldn't do otherwise.

I stopped by the room where she was lying. She was still in the bed, with her eyes closed, just as I left her. She was as beautiful as ever. I wanted to stay by her side, but she wasn't alive, yet. I brushed a kiss on her cold hand, murmuring a soft promise to her, "Just a little longer, we'll be together again."

I didn't want to leave her side, but a warning from the demon was enough to convince me to exit the room.

"Don't forget the invasion."

I grunted at the demon and got to the rest of the castle. My servants had done well. They had cleaned up the dust and spider webs. The castle started to look like something that would please Leila.

I went to the portal in the throne room. The centaur general was there.

"Report," I ordered, annoyed by this war.

The centaur slightly bowed before answering, "Everything is going well, master. We control most of the major cities. We kill anyone who will not bow to us. All is going according to plan."

This invasion was futile. I didn't care about it one bit.

"But I care about it! Remember our bargain," Eurynomos spoke angrily.

"Speaking of our bargain. I have the Desire's Etcher. It's time for you to hold up your end of the bargain and revive her."

I could feel that Eurynomos was irritated inside of me.

"I can't revive her, yet."

I yelled, "What? You told me to retrieve the dagger. I have it!"

"You need to spawn a tower to drain energy from the livings. Reviving someone requires an

immense amount of energy. But first, in order to spawn the tower, you need to break the dagger so that I can retrieve my powers."

I was beginning to doubt the intentions of the demon, but it was too late now. I would see this through.

I dropped the dagger on the floor. Then, I asked one of the orcs standing nearby to lend me his mace. I hit the dagger with it, with no success. I kept hitting, my forehead sweating from the effort. After a few times, the dagger finally broke in half, the blade separating from the handle. As it did, I felt a dark energy flow through my veins. The power was pouring into me. It was invigorating on a level I never thought possible.
Surely, now I had enough power to spawn the tower Eurynomos was talking about.

"Demon, how do I spawn the tower?"

I could feel the demon grinning inside of me.

"Just concentrate on it. I will do the rest from inside."

I did as the demon asked. I concentrated on spawning a tower, even though I had no idea of how to do so. Pain started to shoot from my body. It felt like my insides were tearing apart. A cry of agony escaped my lips, piercing through the silence of the moment. I could feel Eurynomos working as well. I held my head in my hands, digging my nails into my own skin from the pain. I fell to my knees, consumed by the pain. My head started turning, then everything went black.

I was tired. How many waves had we fought back already? I couldn't keep count. Our soldiers were tired, and so were the dragons. Luckily, Elwin and Ravynne were able to heal the wounded, but I wondered how much time before they couldn't keep up with the pace.

Damien was orchestrating everything, but I could feel his worry through our mate bond. He kept a strong facade, but he couldn't hide it from me. I kept pushing encouragement to him through our mate bond.

It had been a while since Bianca left, and we had heard nothing from them. I only hoped she had succeeded in mastering her powers, so that these attacks would stop soon. Damien was the vampire Lord. Our people counted on us to keep them safe. I wasn't sure how much longer we would be able to do so.

Furthermore, I was worried about Will's pack, my old pack. Were my parents okay? Were they under heavy attack as we were? I only hoped everyone was fine.

I watched helplessly from the balcony as our warriors fought back yet another wave of evil creatures. I wondered how many orcs there could be. It seemed there was no end to their numbers! The same went for goblins, harpies, centaurs, succubi, and other vile demons attacking us.

I was happy that Cain and Zarek were still with us, as they were formidable warriors. They fought by Lilith's side. A pile of corpses forming around them. Damien insisted on fighting by their side, despite the fact it worried me terribly. But he explained he couldn't stay there idly watching the army attacking. He wanted to protect me; his mate. I could totally understand this, as I felt the same way towards him.

The bodies were piling up. The sound of the metal clashing everywhere. The number of enemies was finally reducing, giving me hope that we were winning. The cooks were already preparing stew and blood glasses to replenish our warriors after the wave. They had fought through the night and were surely tired. Hopefully, they would have time to nap before the next wave.

The blinds in the castle had been closed to filter the sun's rising rays, giving a better chance for our soldiers to rest.

The ground shook. I braced the railing as I suddenly felt weak. The castle was soon plunged into obscurity. Afar, a tall, dark structure had risen to the east, completely hiding the sun. It was immense and hid the rising sun, leaving us in the shadows. I looked around in the courtyard, and all the soldiers were now fighting difficultly.

"Are you alright?" I heard through my mate bond.

"I'm feeling weak."

Damien acknowledged what I said, and I could feel his understanding through our bond.

"Same as everyone here. I'm coming."

I went back inside our room and waited for him. I felt too weak to do anything. It took only a few seconds for him to arrive.

"I don't know what this tower is," he started. "But it seems to be draining our soldier's energy. We need to counteract it or else we will fall."

He was seriously worried now. He was always so sure of himself. This couldn't be good.

"What can we do?"

I kept searching in my mind, but other than blowing the tower down, I didn't see what we could do. Damien smiled when he saw what I was thinking through our bond.

His eyes were glowing as he spoke.

"That could work, but first, we need to destroy the current wave of enemies. And I think I know just how to do it."

He grabbed my hand. We rushed to the infirmary to see Elwin and Ravynne.

"Elwin! We need to activate the castle's ancient magic," ordered Damien.

The old sorcerer's mouth went agape.

"Are you sure, my lord? You know what this implies."

"This is a dire situation! We need to, even if it means we might lose some citizens."

I watched both with wide eyes. Ravynne looked at them the same way.

I asked, "Would one of you care to explain to us what's happening?"

They both turned to look at me and Ravynne, as if remembering we were there and didn't know what they were talking about.

"Oh, right," said Damien with a grave tone. "The ancient castle's magic is a powerful shield that is to be enabled only in case of an emergency. But by doing so, it will launch a wave of energy strong enough that it could kill part of the vampires' citizens, or even destroy a part of the city. But given the circumstances... I think it's our only option."

Now I understood the hesitation of Elwin. To protect the castle, at the risk of killing our own people. But given the tower sapping our energy, the never-ending waves, and the tired soldiers, it might very well be our only option.

"Right, I understand," I answered softly.

"What do you think, my little wolf?" Damien asked through our mate bond.

"I think it's a reasonable thing to do, which could allow us to save more lives than lose. Therefore, we should do it," I answered aloud.

Damien smiled at me.

"Thank you, my Queen," he answered, before adding through our mate bond. "Your opinion is most valuable to me. I'm happy to be able to rely on you in this stressful time."

I smiled proudly at his comment, even if I was the only one hearing it.

"Thank you, my love," I whispered back through our mate bond, sending a wave of love his way.

"Let's hurry to the control room." Gestured Elwin.

We all followed him down a stone staircase that I had never seen before. It was in a part of the castle I had never been. Spider webs decorated the walls. As we got down, we saw a strange mechanism controlled by a big crystal crank.

I asked, "Do we need to move this?"

Damien shook his head. "It's activated by magic. We need Elwin and Ravynne to unlock it. Only then will we be able to turn it."

Elwin spoke some words to Ravynne in a tongue I didn't know. Ravynne nodded. I guess it was a magical universal language or something like that. Together, they started chanting words.

"Protegat activate scutum magicae…"

A big clanking sound was heard from the mechanism, as if something unlocked. Damien gestured to me. I started pushing the crank with him, as Ravynne and Elwin continued their chant. The crank started moving, as well as the gears. We kept on pushing until the mechanism came to a stop.

A whooshing sound was heard all around us, and crystals lit up in the ceiling.

Damien was excited. "Let's go see."

We got up as fast as we could. The sound of the battle had stopped. When we looked outside, we could see that the demon's army was dead. Our soldiers were standing with a wondering look on their faces. All around the castle was a big bubble of energy. It was sparking every time an enemy, or the dark energy from the tower to the East, was trying to hit it. This allowed me to see the glowing edge of the otherwise invisible bubble. The feeling of energy drain was also gone. I was feeling better again.

"It worked!" exclaimed Elwin in awe.

The soldiers were already coming back inside to eat and rest, as the enemies were gone.

"Great! Let's take care of our soldiers, then," I said eagerly.

"Yes, then we'll see what we can do to get rid of this tower. We can't keep the protection shield on all the time. It will eventually run out of energy," said, Damien.

I looked at him, worried. I had no idea it was a temporary thing. Then we needed to find a solution and fast. But at least, this was buying us some time.

*********** Blake's POV ***********

I was eating supper in the company of Zach and Eshenesra. The food was great. I hadn't told her what I had asked of the King and Queen. I hoped she wouldn't be angry with me. I will tell her when I'd be alone with her. For now, I was happy to watch how fast she had become friends with Zach. She was smiling and talking lively. It was as if she was a completely different person from the person she was before. It filled my heart with joy to see her like that.

I fought with my instincts that were telling me to claim her. It was getting harder with every passing hour. I took a glass of blood wine to try to calm the beast inside of me. I was a dark heritage of the vampires that growled inside of me from time to time, requiring me to claim the woman I loved. It was driving me crazy. I knew she was my mate. I hoped she felt the same about me as well.

Bianca, Steven, Arius, and Elashor walked into the room. Arius was carrying a big box.
"Hi everyone!" said Bianca, cheerfully.
"Welcome back!" I answered.
"How was the training?" asked Eshenesra.
"Great! Iain said that I'm ready."
This was good news. I knew we needed to go soon. And from what Zach had told me, this wouldn't be an easy fight.
"What's with the big box?" asked Zach.

A metallic sound echoed as Arius placed the box on the floor. He grinned, looking at us.
"Kõrvits sends his regards."
He proceeded to open the box and got a small machine out of it.
"What is this?" I asked curiously.
The box contained dozens of them. I picked one of them up in my hand. It was about the size of

my hand. It had propellers on top and carried arrows.

Arius answered, "Kõrvits called this a warkot. It's a flying machine spitting arrows at enemies."

I watched the machine in my hand, impressed.

I exclaimed, "That's amazing! Did he have those in his store?"

Elashor nodded. "Remember when he said he used to travel with his friends? It was one of the types of robots he used to make. He had a bunch of them lying around in a box."

Steven added, "When we told him we needed to fight off a demon, he immediately insisted that we take them."

"Especially after I told him how much I loved the pocket cuckoo he gave me," added Elashor, smiling.

"What about you guys?" asked Arius.

Zach got the vial of poison from his pocket.

"Eshenesra brought us to the underground market. We got this poison."

Everyone stared at the black vial.

"It's supposed to be very potent," added Zach.

"That will surely be useful," said, Bianca.

Just as we spoke, the floor shook, causing the chandeliers to sway and destabilizing the frames. We all stared at each other, wondering what had just happened. Castle guards came into the room, searching for what might be threatening the castle.

"What the hell was that?" asked Bianca.

Arius was about to say something when a portal opened out of thin air. Iain exited from it, worried.

"I felt a strong magical wave coming from the West. I figured I should come and see you."

"We were just talking about it," answered Bianca.

"The castle is in danger," said Arius with a serious tone.

"This castle?" asked Eshenesra, worried. I grabbed her hand and squeezed it.

"No," answered Arius. "The vampire's castle is in danger. This is an ancient protection magic hidden in the castle. It's supposed to be used only in a last resort situation."

Eshenesra seemed relieved by his answer. The elven castle was her home. At least, it used to be, but she didn't know it yet.

"We need to get back to my castle, and fast!" stated Arius.

He was about to go when Iain stopped him.

"Let me go with you. I can open a portal to the castle. It will be faster than walking there."

Arius smiled at the mage.

"That would be great! But we have no idea of what's awaiting. Are you seriously ready to put your life at risk without knowing what we'll be facing?"

Iain nodded to him. "Sure. It sounds fun!"

"Okay, then open up a portal so that we can cross."

Elashor spoke, "Don't you even think of leaving without me!"

Arius turned to her and smiled, "I wouldn't dare, my love." He kissed her tenderly.

I was torn. As a loyal guard of Damien, I felt obligated to go back to the castle to help. But at the same time, I didn't want to leave Eshenesra. And there was still this matter of fighting off Will. I stared at Eshenesra, then at Arius, who was smiling at me.

He grinned at me. "You should stay here, Blake. Help with the fight against the demon. I'll protect the castle with Damien."

Relief filled me at those words. The smirk he had on his face led me to think he suspected something about Eshenesra and me. I couldn't tell him how grateful I was. I only bowed my head. "As you wish, my prince."

Zach told them, "Please, take care of yourselves." The three of them nodded before stepping inside the portal.

I watched everyone. It was time that we prepared for our journey. I spoke out loud what everyone was thinking. "We should get going, too. Let's end this war."

They all nodded at me, but Eshenesra's eyes darkened. She looked sad. That's when I realized I needed to tell her. But before I had the chance to, a castle's servant interrupted.

"Miss Eshenesra? The King and the Queen wish to see you, now."

She turned her head towards me. "You're not going before I get the chance to say bye, are you?"

I grinned. "Don't you worry about that."

She smiled, relieved, and followed the servant to the throne room. I smiled. I knew what the King and the Queen were about to tell her.

"How are we going to carry these?" asked Zach, pointing to the flying robot box.

"I guess we could split them across the bags on our horses," proposed Steven.

"That sounds like a good idea," I answered.

We prepared the bags and supplies for the trip to come and secured them on the horses.

Chapter 12 (Blake)

Eshenesra came to join us a few minutes later. She looked shocked. I grabbed her hand softly.

"What is the matter?" I asked gently.

She stared into my eyes.

"The king and the queen… They said I should come with you."

I smiled at her words. So, they haden't told her I was the one that requested she leave with me. I was hoping they wouldn't tell her. I wanted them to keep our conversation private.

When I asked her if she could come with me, they asked me why. They were horrified when I told them how Scalanis was treating her. They had no idea he was beating her. They only thought he was harsh with her, from time to time, but never that it was that bad. They immediately accepted my request, promising to make sure Scalanis doesn't beat anyone else. Scalanis was demoted, and now had to follow the orders of another one. They already named a new chief for the servant's quarters. It wouldn't change what he did to Eshenesra, but it was satisfying knowing he wasn't in charge anymore. Of course, if it were up to me, I would have done much worse to him.

I smiled at Eshenesra.

"I'm happy that they asked you to come with us."

She smiled back. "I'm a little shocked, but I'm happy, too."

I gestured to her. "We don't have enough horses for everyone. You should ride on my horse with me. Would that be okay?" She studied me, then nodded.

I helped her up onto my horse, then I sat behind her. The feeling of having her so close to me was driving me crazy. The warmth of her body against mine felt like paradise.

She laid her back against my chest as we started to ride. The horse's movement made her hips sway in a sensual way, making me yearn for her. Her neck was so close to me that I could almost brush my teeth on her skin, feeling her vein pulsing as blood passed through. She was tantalizing, and I struggled to resist her. Her irresistible scent of peaches and spices was intoxicating. I had to fight my vampiric instincts that wanted to take control of me.

It would take us a few days to get to Darton Castle. I never imagined what a sweet torture these travel days would be. To have her so close to me, yet out of reach. To have my heart racing for this sweet temptress, my fiery flower of desire. I needed to calm myself down and control my instincts. I couldn't allow myself to take her in front of everyone.

"I still don't understand why the King and the Queen asked me to come with you."

My heart was beating fast. I didn't know how to tell her. Would she be happy, or would she hate me for taking her away from her life? I didn't even ask her if she wanted to come with me.

"Well, I have to confess that it's because of me."

"What?"

"It's because of me that the King and the Queen asked you to come with me."

She turned her head to look at me with wide eyes as the horse kept on walking. "How so?"

I didn't want to tell her that I spoke about the fact Scalanis was beating her. I was sure she wouldn't be okay with this. But I couldn't stand by and do nothing, knowing how she was being treated. That, and the fact that I loved her, and I couldn't bear the thought of losing her. Yet, somehow, I didn't know how to express these feelings to her. I've never experienced anything like this. A sword fight was so much easier. I felt lost, not knowing what to do with these emotions that were overwhelming with me.

The simplest thing I could do was come up with a stupid explanation. "I told them I wanted to eat well while we traveled."

I regretted saying this the moment I did. It was stupid, but it was the first idea that came to my mind. The look of disappointment on her face made my heart sink. "Oh… Is that all? You want to eat well while you travel?"

She looked hurt, and I felt like the worst idiot that ever existed. My heart was hammering in my chest. I needed to come clean about how I felt with her.

"The truth is, I couldn't even think of leaving without you. I'm sorry. It was selfish. I hope you can forgive me. I thought only of my feelings, and how I need to have you close to me. I couldn't bear to be without you."
She stared at me with wide eyes. Those seconds of silence seemed like an eternity. I waited anxiously for her answer. Finally, she smiled and snuggled closer to me. A sense of relief took over me when she whispered, "Thank you."

I wrapped my arms around her while holding the horse's bridle. My heart was hammering in my chest. She was too tempting. I leaned forward and kissed her neck, my lips lingering on her skin. She turned her head towards me, smiling. She closed her eyes as her lips met mine, her hand landing on my chest. A deep rumble reverberated through my chest.

She whispered, "I was so scared that you would leave, and I would never see you again."

Just the thought of it was unbearable. I squeezed her in my arms. "I could never do that!"

We rode in silence for a while. I could smell the scent of death as we passed villages. The demon's army was gone. There was nothing left. Houses were destroyed, farms were burned. Everything had been destroyed. They probably went on to fight the next town. It was a sad sight.

The few remaining survivors were searching through the rubble, trying to find something to salvage from the carnage. In some places, big piles of corpses were burning. The smell was nauseatingly sweet, something like flame-tanned leather with a hint of copper and sulfur. The smell was so thick and rich that I could almost taste it.

We decided to get away from the main roads and to return to the woods. We wanted to avoid meeting the demon's army at all costs. Our focus was to get to Eurynomos as fast as possible and end this carnage.

As we rode, a big dragon flew over our heads. It was so low that the wind from the dragon's wings was tearing the leaves off the trees. We stopped for a moment to admire the magnificence of the beast. A man was riding on his back. I heard him shout, "Higher, Sozar. We need to get to Eiyrăl." The dragon flapped its wing a few times, gaining in altitude, flying swiftly through the air.

Soon, they were far enough you could think it was only a huge bird.

We soon arrived at the edge of the woods. Further, we could see plains, then a bridge.

"We should set up camp here for the night," stated Zach.

"We could still ride for an hour or two," argued Steven.

"True, but it would be safer to camp in the woods rather than in the plains."

He was right. We got down from our horses and set up the camp. The elven king and queen had given us plenty of supplies. I had already eaten supper, but Bianca and Steven hadn't got the chance before we left. We talked around the fire while Bianca and Steven ate. Eshenesra was cuddling with me, and I couldn't be happier. It was already late, so we decided to call it a day.

As I laid in my tent with Eshenesra, I couldn't fall asleep. This was too much for me. I couldn't fight it anymore. I needed to claim her. It was an urge, so strong, I couldn't hold it any longer.

I could feel she wasn't sleeping either.

I whispered in a husky voice, "Eshenesra, there is something I need to tell you."

Her yellow eyes glowed in the dark as she turned around, staring at me.

"Yes, Blake?"

Her voice was soft and melodious.

"I tried to fight it so much, but it's of no use."

"To fight what?"

I swallowed hard.

"To fight these feelings that I have for you. But I can't! I need to say it."

She pleaded, "Please don't!"

I looked up at her, surprised, "Why?"

Her voice was but a murmur, "Because if you leave me, I'll get hurt."

My heart sank at those words.

"Eshenesra, I will never leave you. Don't you see? You're the fire that fuels my soul. You're my mate. I will be with you, forever."

I could hear Eshenesra's heartbeat increasing.

"Your… mate?"

"Yes, my mate. The one made especially for me, as I was made for you. I will be yours forever."

Her eyes searched my soul, her heart synched with mine.

"Do you promise?"

I nodded, looking her straight in the eyes.

"I do. I love you more than words can express, Eshenesra."

She smiled.

"I love you too, Blake."

Those words were too good to be true. Like a heartfelt confession spoken after being kept secret for too long.

My lips devoured hers with passion while I caressed her body softly. Her body responded to mine, her hips softly rocking against mine.

I asked her, breathless, "Please, won't you let me claim you?"

"Claim me? What does it mean?"

"It's something we vampires do. It means… It means that I get to share my deepest feelings with you. To love you, body and soul. To make love to you… and to drink your blood."

Worry flashed in her eyes.

"You want to drink my blood?"

"I've been yearning for you so much. It's hurting me. But don't worry, I won't hurt you. I'll only drink a little bit of it. I swear it won't hurt."

I could see she was debating whether she should do this or not.

"Are you sure it won't hurt?"

"Positive. This bite will seal the bond between us. Making you mine, as I am yours. I promise you'll enjoy this."

She smiled.

"This sounds beautiful."

"Of course. I don't want to force this on you. This is the most intimate bond vampires can share. Our souls will be woven together forever. We might even be able to share our thoughts."

Instead of answering, Eshenesra started kissing me, her jewel shining brightly on her chest. Her kiss was passionate and needy, our tongues dancing together. A deep purr escaped my chest as her hands started to roam my body. Her hands were so warm compared to me. A groan escaped my lips. I've been longing for this for such a long time, I struggled to keep my instincts under control.

I took a deep breath of her scent of peach and spices. She was my heaven. I bit her bottom lip slightly, earning a small moan from her. Her voice sounded like the sweetest music to my ears. A fire ignited inside of me as my fingers brushed against her soft skin.

I got on top of her and started to remove her clothes, kissing every inch of her body as I did. Her moans were my guide to exactly where and how to touch her. The scent of her arousal was getting me hard.

"Hm… Blake," she moaned sensually as I rubbed my finger over her clit.

I kissed her as I kept my endeavors, bringing her over the edge, her legs shaking. It was the most beautiful sight ever, to see the woman I loved blossom under my touch.

"Please, take me," she begged.

I smiled; she wouldn't have to ask me twice. I took off my clothes. She was devouring me with her eyes, and I couldn't wait to give her what she wanted.

She was dripping wet from her earlier orgasm. I aligned myself with her and started to thrust into her. I couldn't hold a groan as she was so tight and warm around me.

My instincts soon took a hold of me, urging me to make her mine.

I licked the skin of her neck, and my fangs grew. I could easily feel her blood pulsing in her veins. She arched her back and pressed her nails into my back as I bit her. I lost control of my body the moment her blood hit my tongue. This was the sweetest, most perfect nectar I had ever drunk. Her moans intensified, and she screamed, "Yes!" as I drank her blood.

I could feel her pleasure, inside and out. I was drowning in an ocean of bliss. I was lost in her, and never wanted to come back.

I thrust harder and soon felt her walls pulse around me. I held her hips as I thrust a few more times deeper, trembling as I came in my turn. I slowly removed my fangs from her neck, letting my tongue linger on the spot to heal the wound.

When I finally looked back into her eyes, I could see my future in them. She was smiling in a way I have never seen her smile yet. The jewel on her chest was glowing and pulsing.

"Blake, that was… amazing!" she whispered to me.

I couldn't help but to feel proud with her words.

"Eshenesra, you are the only one for me. You're my heaven, the fire that lights my soul. I will always be there for you."

She smiled. "I know. I could feel it all when you bit me."

I was glad she was able to feel it.

"Then it means the bond works."

She pointed at the jewel, still pulsing, embedded in her chest.

"I can feel you inside of me, here."

I smiled and put my hand over her pulsing jewel. It felt warm to the touch.

"That's good. That way, you'll never feel lonely again."

When I bit her through our bond, I had felt all her past sadness and worries. I had seen how lonely she had been. How vulnerable she was when she was beaten. I was happy to know she wouldn't feel like that again. I would make sure to fill her days with joy as much as I could.

"I love you," Eshenesra whispered into my mind.

Her eyes widened with the realization she had spoken into my mind.

"Our bond will only grow stronger with time," I whispered back into her mind.

I kissed her sweet lips another time. I couldn't believe how precious this woman was to me.

I murmured softly, "I love you, my sweet angel."

She cuddled in my arms, her hot breath brushing on my chest as we fell asleep.

*********** Kate's POV ************

Just as we were walking towards the castle, we heard a big whooshing sound. Soldiers braced themselves as a portal opened into thin air in the castle's courtyard. From the portal came Arius, Elashor, and an elven man dressed in a mage's robe.

"Arius? Elashor? What are you doing here?" I asked in disbelief.

"You activated the castle's ancient magic. I knew you needed some help," stated Arius.

Damien grinned. "I knew I could count on you, brother."

The two of them hugged. Arius presented the mage to us.

"Damien, Kate, meet Iain. He's the magic guild's high mage."

I gasped at his words. "You mean?"

He nodded. "That's right. He's the one who trained Bianca."

My sister! How I missed her. It felt like I hadn't seen her in forever.

"Tell me, how is she?"

Iain had a mysterious smile as he answered, "She's ready."

This only meant she was probably on her way to fight Eurynomos. Or maybe she was already there. A knot formed in my stomach at the thought of my sister fighting this demon. I knew she was the Moon Goddess's daughter. I knew she was strong. But I was scared, nonetheless.

Arius had an uneasy look on his face.

"We also… had an encounter… with Will."

"An encounter? What do you mean?" I asked.

Elashor glanced at him for a second before he spoke more.

"He… sided with the demon."

Wait what? Did I hear that right? This couldn't be! "That can't be! The demon killed his mate! It's impossible."

Elashor nodded sadly.

Arius replied, "We fought with him. He's very powerful now that he's merged with the demon. He injured us quite direly. We were saved by the magic guild's potions."

I fell to my knees, tears rolling down my cheeks. My world crumbled to pieces. How could my brother merge with a terrible demon? Especially the one who killed his mate? This didn't make sense!

Damien pulled me into his arms. Wrapped in his love, I let my tears flow. I couldn't believe what my brother had done. Yet, it was true.
Will was so strong as an Alpha. I couldn't even imagine how strong he was now that he had merged with Eurynomos.

I whispered to Damien, "Do you think they'll make it?"

His gray eyes stared into mine.

"Bianca and Steven? Of course, they will! Don't forget, Blake and Zach are there with them as well."

Arius added, "Eshenesra as well."

We all turned to him. Damien asked, "Eshenesra?"

Arius nodded and smirked. "Yes. She's Blake's mate. Well, he hasn't said so, but it's easy to see."

So, they were five… but I was still worried Will was stronger than them.

"I think we should send them the dragons."
They all looked at me.

I continued, "I think they need them more than us. It will be useful to fight against the demon."

Damien landed a soft kiss on my lips, setting fire to my heart.

"As you wish, my wise queen."

I smiled and kissed him back. He was my force, my confidence. I loved him with all that I was.

I walked towards the dragons. Ladon raised one of his heads, staring at me as I approached. I got close to him, staring at him. I wasn't sure how to speak to a dragon. I wasn't sure they would understand me. My wolf started to stir inside of me, and I could feel that she was trying to speak to the dragon.

Softly, I whispered, "Please, you must go join with Bianca and the others. You need to help them fight off the demon."

There was a moment of hesitation. I could feel my wolf talking with the dragon. I could understand it clearly. Will was Ladon's Alpha. He wanted to obey to Will, and no one else. My wolf explained to him, Will had sided with the demon. He wasn't his master anymore. We needed their help if we were to try to save my brother from the demon. After a moment, Ladon seemed to agree with my request.

He got up and growled loudly at the other dragons. They all got up and growled in response to their leader. Ladon turned towards me and nodded. Together, they flew up to the sky and started to make their way north-east. I had no idea how they would be able to know where to find Bianca. I only hoped their instincts or magic would guide them.

When I joined the others, they were talking lively. Damien was giving orders to soldiers in the courtyard.

"What's happening?" I asked them.

Damien grinned.

"Well, we still need to deal with this tower; before the castle's protection wears off."

Right, I had almost forgotten about that. Just when I was about to answer something, my legs felt weak. I almost fell to the floor, but Damien picked me up quickly. He took me in his strong arms, squeezing me lovingly.

"Are you alright, my little wolf?"

His voice was full of worry.

"Yes, I'm just tired, I guess. And hungry."

"Well, then, maybe you should stay at the castle while we deal with the tower."

I protested, "What? No way! I want to come with you guys!"

Elashor smiled at me. "I know you want to come. But maybe you should rest?"

I frowned, still in Damien's arms.

"If another wave hits us, staying at the castle is as dangerous as going to the tower. Besides, I don't want to stay here alone."

Damien studied me. I pushed through his mind, "You know I won't back down."

He sighed and answered through our bond, "I know, but I'm worried about you, my little wolf."

"I'll be fine," I answered out loud.

Damien took a moment, then replied, "Okay, but not before we've eaten, and not before you get a resistance potion from Elwin."

I nodded to him. A resistance potion was probably for the best.

We all got inside the castle and ate a hearty meal. I hadn't realized how hungry I was. Being pregnant was getting me to eat way more than usual. I felt better once I had eaten.

"Let's get a resistance potion," stated Arius. When we got to the courtyard, we found Elwin and Ravynne holding hands lovingly together. It was sweet to see their love blossom.

"Well, what do you know?" said Arius. "I've never seen the old sorcerer so happy. Nice for them!"

We walked to them. "Elwin," started Damien. "We need resistance potions. One especially strong for Kate."

Elwin bowed his head to Damien. "Of course, my Lord."

We followed him into the castle, to his laboratory. He searched through his chests and got a few purple vials. One of them was darker than the others.

"Here you go." He handed the potions to Damien. Then he handed me the darker one.

"This one is for you, my queen."

Iain grabbed one of the potions, studying it carefully.

"Very impressive, my friend," he commented.

Elwin smiled. "Maybe we should invite mage guests to the castle more often. They're the only ones who really appreciate my work."

Damien laughed at his comment. "Come on, my friend. Do you really believe we don't appreciate your work?"

Elwin grinned. "No, of course, I don't. I was just joking."

Damien smiled. "You are welcome to invite mages at the castle as you wish. Just make sure to tell me or Kate about it, so that we're aware of it."

Elwin bowed his head. "Thank you, my lord."

Everyone drank their potions. I removed the lid off mine. It smelled like aged wine. But I knew it didn't contain any alcohol. I drank it in one sip. I had to refrain from spitting it out. It tasted awful! Like warm red wine left sitting on a counter all day. But I knew it was for my own good, so I swallowed it all.

I stared at everyone. We all had the same face. We thanked Elwin for the potions but didn't say anything about the taste. Elashor only spoke when we left his laboratory, exclaiming, "Well… that was something!"

We all laughed at her comment. We didn't need her to say anything more. We knew what she meant.

Chapter 13 (Kate)

We got back to the courtyard. Lilith was instructing the troops.

"Lilith!" Damien called.

She met with us. "Yes, my Lord."

"We're leaving to take care of the tower to the east. Please protect the castle."

She put a hand on her heart. "I won't fail you."

Damien smiled. "I know you won't."

We all turned our heads suddenly, when an old vampire landed just beside us. Lilith drew her sword, but Damien gestured for her not to.

He looked at the vampire and asked, "You're not one of my subjects. Who are you?"

I was relieved when the vampire bowed his head, recognizing Damien's rank.

"Please excuse my intrusion. I was called here by Cain."

Damien raised his brow. "Cain?"

A bulky man came towards us, smiling.

"Vlad! You made it!"

The vampire smiled at the werewolf.

"Of course, I came as soon as I got your text."

I looked at them, confused. "Will one of you explain what's going on?"

"Of course, your Majesty," the werewolf answered. "Me and Zarek over there. We were talking, and I thought we could use more help. So I texted Vlad and asked him to help."

I looked at them. They only wanted to help, and the vampire did feel like he was very powerful.

I pushed through Damien's mind, "What do you think?"

He answered, "As long as they obey our general, I don't mind having more people helping."

I nodded to Cain. "Thank you for having your friend to help us."

He grinned. "He's good to help everyone. He always helps us in the support groups."

I wasn't sure what he meant about a support group, but as long as he helped, I was fine with it.

Damien added, "I expect each and every one of you to obey the orders of our general, Lilith, while I'm gone."

Vlad, Cain, Zarek, and all the soldiers gestured that they would. I felt at peace, leaving the castle well-guarded.

As we exited the protection bubble of the castle, thousands of corpses laid on the ground. They had likely been killed by the spell we activated earlier. I repressed the need to vomit from the putrid smell that was coming from the decaying corpses. In the sky, the tower was launching magic attacks at the protection bubble. It made a zapping sound, and I could see the bubble lighting up with each strike. I immediately felt weaker than inside the castle, but Elwin's resistance potion lessened the effects of the tower on me. Damien grabbed my hand, intertwining his fingers with mine.

He spoke with a strong voice as we started walking east, "Let us make haste and get rid of this tower."

************ Eshenesra's POV ************

I woke up in Blake's arms. He was still sleeping. My heart fluttered at the thought of what happened yesterday. Never in my life have I felt so loved. When he drank my blood, I saw it all. I saw his life as a human, his death, and his transformation. I saw how he lost everyone he loved, and how he built himself a shell. More importantly, I felt how much he loved me. He loved me so much that his shell shattered when he met me. Now, he feared losing me, and he would give his life to protect me. I had no doubt in my mind; I wanted to stay with him forever.

The sound of the others talking outside came into our tent. We would need to get up soon and leave. The journey ahead of us scared me. But we were a team now. I wasn't alone. Blake started to stir in his sleep. I brushed my fingers on his chest. His lips curved upward, and he opened his eyes.

"Good morning, my beautiful mate," he said softly.

I kissed his delicious lips, our tongues dancing together. He wrapped his arms around me, bringing me closer to him.

"Hm… You're the most delicious thing to wake up to."

I smiled at his comment. I was about to answer when a sound from outside the tent reached us.

"Hey Steven, get the breakfast ready while I pack my things."

I sighed and whispered to Blake, "I guess we should join them."

He chuckled softly, "Yes, I guess you're right."

We got up. I spied on Blake's naked body as he got dressed. He was so perfect! I could admire him for hours.

He smirked. "You should get those thoughts under control, or we'll never leave."

I blushed and got dressed quickly. He kissed me one more time before we exited the tent.

"Good morning, you two!" said Bianca, with a big smile.

"Good morning!" I replied, before joining her.

Blake started to pack our tent. Zach soon joined him to help. In no time, all the tents were packed. The horses had fresh hay to feed on while we ate breakfast.

The plan for today was clear: cross over that bridge that we saw yesterday and try to get to the castle where Will was hiding. This would be tricky. Past the woods, we saw only plains and farmland. This meant that we would be moving in plain sight. We needed to move quickly and hope we wouldn't attract too much attention. The tension was palpable as we prepared for the journey ahead of us.

************ Bianca's POV ************

We rode in silence. I had so many questions at the same time. Would we reach the castle tonight? How would my brother react when he sees me? Would we be able to save him from the demon? Would I be able to fight off Eurynomos? What if Iain was wrong? What if I wasn't ready? I prayed to the Moon Goddess that I would be strong enough and that she would help me.

Birds flew away as we passed nearby through the plains. There was an eerie silence around us. The demon's army had come and killed everything. Only a few birds remained, and they stood silent, for fear of attracting the orcs. The tall grass swayed in the wind. I held my breath when, from time to time, something moved in the grass under the vibration of the horses' hooves. Luckily, it was surely a snake or a rodent running away.

We quickly arrived at a wide wooden bridge. It looked sturdy enough for all of us to pass. On the other side were farmlands. No enemies were in sight.

"Let's go in single file. It will even out the weight on the bridge," suggested Steven.

We all nodded. Steven was the first to go, and I followed him. I stared at the violent waters of the river. The waves crushed against rocks as if the water itself was angry about the events to come. We waited for everyone to cross, then ventured into the farmlands. The lands were narrow, and we could already see another river waiting on the other side.

"There's no bridge," I declared.

We studied the lands.

"If we go west, we'll eventually get back to the pack," Steven commented.

"That's the opposite of the way we need to go," added, Blake.

Which only left us with the option of going east. There used to be a farm to the east, but now there were only the remains of it. It was probably raided by the demon's army a few days ago.

We made our way towards the farm, hoping to find a way to cross over the river. As we arrived near the burned building, I noticed a small house made of loose rocks and mud. It didn't even have a front door or windows. There were holes to allow someone to come inside and out of the house.

I whispered to Steven, "Do you think someone still lives in there?"

"Could anyone even live in such a rundown house? It doesn't even have proper walls."

Just as we passed in front of the house, an old woman came out of it. Her white hair was long enough to go down her back. Her fingers were bony, and she looked like she hadn't been properly eating in a while. Something was wrong with her, but I couldn't put my finger on it.

"Why, hello there! We don't get a lot of visitors over here."

Her voice was high pitched. She looked frail, but she still made the hairs on the back of my neck stand up. I could feel that Steven's wolf was feeling uneasy through our bond.

"Nice to meet you," I answered politely.

"Would one of you young men please help an old lady?"

"Sure," answered Blake while getting off his horse. "What can I do to help you?"

As he asked this, the old lady's head tilted sideways, and her eyes became empty. She hissed and jumped on Blake, all nails out, trying to bite him. We got off our horses to try to help him, but he didn't need our help. In one big push, he got her off him.

"What the hell is wrong with her?" he shouted.

We tried to approach her, but she started talking in a language we didn't know, black blood leaking from her mouth. As she did, a dark energy surrounded her, dust raising from the ground.

"She's been tainted by demon blood!" Zach shouted. "Be careful. She might summon the dead to fight."

Just as he said that, four bodies rose from the ground. They had been mutilated and one of them was even missing an arm. But it didn't seem to hinder their will to fight.

Eshenesra's horse neighed with fear, rearing on its back legs. Eshenesra pulled on the reins and managed to get the horse back down. All the horses were getting uneasy as the dead bodies started walking towards them.

Eshenesra yelled through the chaos, "I'll get a little further away with the horses, so they don't run away."

Zach started to fight one of the bodies with his sharp claws, and to attack another one with his favorite levitating sword. Steven and I each took one of the bodies. Meanwhile, Blake was trying to push through the dark wind to get to the old lady. A shadowy figure was now slowly rising from the ground. An aura of power could be felt all the way through me; this couldn't be good.

"Don't let her finish her spell!" I shouted at Blake.

The animated body wasn't fast, but I was surprised by its strength. I summoned a flame and set fire to the one I was fighting. My nose twitched at the smell of burning flesh. I watched in satisfaction as the body burned, the flesh turning to black, before he fell to the floor. Just as I was about to burn the other bodies, the one I just 'killed' got back up again.

"It's not working!" I shouted to the others. "You kill them, and they get back up!"

Zach shouted back, "Yes, I noticed! I cut mine's head off, but he put it back on. We need the old woman dead."

I shouted at Blake, "We'll keep the bodies occupied! Hurry!"

He shouted back, "I'm trying!"

The wall of dark energy around the woman was thick. Blake was struggling to get inside. The shadowy figure was now taller, and I feared the moment when it would be fully summoned.

Screaming in agony, Blake finally succeeded in breaching the dark energy wall. He jumped on the old lady, disrupting her spell. She struggled to get Blake off her, but he wouldn't let her win that easily. Blake grabbed his sword and swung with force at her neck. Her eyes went wide as in one swing, he cut her head off, her mouth stuck in a surprised expression forever.

The dark wind suddenly died. A sense of relief washed over me when the figure that was being summoned disappeared.

The old lady's body started to burn with black flames, consumed by the darkness of the demon that had tainted her. I turned my head when I heard the sound of falling rocks. The house where the old lady was living suddenly collapsed on itself and became a pile of rubble.

We all stood there, catching our breath.

"Well, I surely wasn't expecting this!" exclaimed Blake. "I will think twice before helping an old lady."

We all laughed at his comment.

"You couldn't have known she was possessed," I told him.

"True." He winked.

"Hey! Look at that!" shouted Eshenesra.

We all turned to look at what Eshenesra was pointing at. To the north-east, beyond the burned farm, stood a bridge. A strange aura emanated from it. It was tall and made of dark rocks. Some of them were floating in the air, as if held in place by a dark power. Just looking at the bridge made me shiver. The bridge went up a mountain where laid a castle. The castle where Will was residing. The castle was dark, with high towers.

Although it looked like it was abandoned, I could see succubi flying over it.

We all started walking towards the bridge. A growl echoed in the air. I looked up and saw dragons coming our way.

"They're back!" said Blake happily.

Ladon was flying close to Clara, taking the lead, protecting his lover with his body. Following them were the three other dragons.

I asked in disbelief, "What are they doing here?"

Blake grinned. "I guess they came to help."

Zach suggested, "Maybe Ladon wants to save his master."

I was full of hope at those words. I whispered to myself, "We'll save you, Will."

We continued our way towards the bridge; the dragons flying near us. Together, we formed a strong team. I was confident more than ever that we'd save my brother.

The bridge was long and steep, but we got to the edge of it. Just being close to the castle, you could feel a wicked energy. Will was surely there, as the castle was heavily protected. Gargoyles and succubi protected the air. In front of the castle was a horde of orcs, centaurs, and lower demons. Goblin mages seemed to be casting spells. A thread of dark energy seemed to link the castle to a tower that had spawned to the south-west. A moat full of sharpened stakes forced everyone to enter the castle by the only rocky path. There seemed to be a bubble of energy encircling the castle.

"What is that?" asked Blake.

I cautiously took a step on the path and stepped inside the bubble. As soon as I did, I could feel my magic being emptied. Panicking, I took a step back.

"It saps magical powers. I can't use magic inside of this bubble."

Blake cursed. Zach pointed towards the goblins. "It's probably cast by those mages."

*********** Eshenesra's POV ***********

"How are we going to defeat them?" asked Bianca. "I can't get in there."

"Neither can we," added Zach. "Blake and I both have magic."

"Well, I can get in there!" spoke Steven. "My wolf and I won't likely get affected by this spell drain." I added, "So can I. I was born without magic."

Blake grabbed my arms. "Please don't go. I would die if something were to happen to you."

I smiled at him. "We're all risking our lives to stop this demon. It's only natural that I help."

"We won't be alone," added Steven. He pointed to the sky. "The dragons will be with us as well."

Blake still had an uneasy look on his face, but nodded, anyway. Reluctantly, he spoke, "Alright, but I would still feel better if we were all together to fight."

"Don't worry," I answered. "I'm good at stalking. If Steven and the dragons distract the fighters, I can easily get to the goblins and eliminate them quickly. You guys will be able to join the fight."

"That sounds like a great plan!" said Bianca. We all agreed to the plan. Even the dragons seemed to understand.

Steven started to advance towards the castle with the dragons. I stood behind them. All my life I had been used to staying in the shadows and going unnoticed. Today, it would finally be useful. I could feel this thick, dark energy surrounding us, but I was unaffected by it. I waited for the first enemies to start attacking Steven and the dragons. The dragons were fighting both enemies in the air and blowing fire to enemies on the ground. Steven was in his wolf's form. He was strong, but I wanted to make haste. I was afraid he would quickly get overrun if I didn't hurry.

Clinging to the shadows, I easily got to the inner walls of the castle. Five goblin mages were busy casting a spell. They were alone, as the others were fighting in front of the castle. I got my dagger out, coating it with a vial of poison I had bought earlier at the underground market.

Sneaking up behind the first goblin, I slit his throat easily, gripping his body so that it didn't fall to the floor. He didn't scream or move. The other goblins were so concentrated on their spells that they didn't even flinch. I slowly got his body down on the floor, then coated my blade in poison again.

I snuk up behind the second goblin and slit his throat as well. The goblin had the time to emit a slight shriek before dying. My heart started beating faster as the other goblins opened their eyes and noticed me. The dead body fell to the floor, as I quickly plunged towards the third goblin, digging my blade into his heart. The goblin fell backwards to the floor, and I fell over him. I kept digging, and turning the blade inside of him, slashing at his internal organs.

The other goblins were trying to pull me off the goblin, scratching at my back, but I kept slashing until he wasn't moving anymore. I finally got up, my back hurting from the attacks of the goblins. They were screaming things at me in a language I didn't understand.

I took a fighting stance, noticing the dark energy was gone. I smiled. This meant the others were on their way to help with the fight. Just as I was preparing to attack the two remaining goblins, a searing pain spread through my back. Sharp claws had sunk into me and were beginning to lift me into the sky. I looked up to see a succubus smiling wickedly at me. I wanted to get off, but I was soon high enough in the sky that I would get crushed if I was to be dropped.

At the top of my lungs, I screamed, "Blake!"

Chapter 14 (Blake)

The Tower

We crossed the bridge as soon as the spell was broken. I rushed towards the castle, slashing through enemies as I did. Around me, blood spilled to the ground, mixed with feathers and flesh. The scream of enemies mixed with ours. I thrived on adrenaline. Battle was my element; I was born to fight. It was even easier now that I was a vampire. A sip of fresh blood would replenish my energy, giving me a second wind to kill off more enemies.

To my left, Zach was killing enemies with his vampire powers and his levitating sword. Bianca was blasting through enemies with her magic. I was impressed with how much she had improved. As for Steven, his wolf's white fur was now tainted with blood from his enemies. He kept biting the flesh off them and snapping their necks. The dragons were decimating enemies from above. Their corpses would come falling like rain. One of them almost hit me. I avoided it at the last moment and the corpse fell on an orc instead.

A scream resonated through my soul, "Blake!"

I turned to look at the castle, my eyes searching for the woman I loved. Following her scream, I finally saw a succubus carrying my sweet Eshenesra into a secondary tower to the right of the castle. Damn! She was way too far for me to do anything.

I pushed through our mate bond, "I'm coming!"

I only hoped she would hear it. Forget the castle and the demon. The only thing that mattered was my mate. I needed to save her. I couldn't bear living without her. A second wave of adrenaline rushed through my veins as I scurried to save my mate.

A swarm of enemies blocked my path, but one by one, I cut them down. Slowly, I made my way towards the tower. I caught a glimpse of the succubus dragging Eshenesra through a window at the top. Wait for me, my love. I'll be there, I promise.

************ Kate's POV ************

I hadn't realized how tall the tower was until we got closer. It was all black and looked like it was made of crystal. The base was wide and steep, like a cliff at least forty feet high. Two demons' heads were carved into the crystal higher. The first one had horns all over his face, his two eyes carving into his face. The second one didn't have horns but had grotesque, pointy teeth sticking out of his mouth. The two of them were staring down at the ground, seemingly looking at anyone who dared to come close to the tower. The top of the tower was shaped in different kinds of horns. Some were twisted spirals, others looked like sword edges. There were six of them in total.

I couldn't imagine anyone building something like this. Only magic could have forged something like that. As we got to the base, a thick magical force filled the air, and I couldn't help but to feel weak, despite the resistance potion Elwin had given me.

"Do you guys feel this?" I asked.

They nodded. "I think it's draining our magic," said Elashor.

"Or our life force," added Iain.

I thought for a minute. "Do you think it's the same kind of spell that got my father bed ridden?"

Damien had a pensive look on his face. "Maybe. I don't know if it's as strong, but it might be related. After all, the magic is likely coming from Eurynomos."

"Right...," I answered. "I hadn't thought of it this way."

The tower had a dark opening at its base. "Any idea how we're going to destroy this thing?" I asked as we scuttled into the dark entrance.

"I'm sure we'll find out," answered Iain. He didn't have time to say anything else before we got attacked by orcs.

"Careful!" yelled Damien before pulling me to his arms just in time to avoid the swing of a sword. The sword cut a hole through my shirt, but I was not hurt. I watched in horror as the sword got lodged into Iain's stomach instead.

"Iain!" I yelled.

Damien was staying in front of me, protecting me from the blows. My wolf was uneasy. She wanted to kill some orcs.

"I want to fight," I pushed through our bond.

"There's no way I'm risking your life and the baby." I could feel through his tone how serious he was. "Take care of Iain instead," he suggested through our bond.

Arius, Elashor, and Damien were fighting off the orcs. I tried to get to Iain through the chaos of the fight, but I couldn't. He kept going deeper into the swarm of enemies. He shot bolts of magic, cutting down enemies as he went, but they kept coming. He looked like he was in some kind of frenzy. He didn't seem to be in his right mind.

At one point, he screamed, "You'll never get me!" before laughing like crazy. A horrible yell resonated as he pulled the sword out of his own stomach. Blood gushed out of his wound, pooling at his feet. A blue energy started to flow from his body, killing off any orcs in proximity, as he grabbed open his wound.

The others stopped fighting and looked on in amazement at this incomprehensible spectacle.
I tried to get to him, but Damien stopped me.
"Iain! Stop! We need to heal you!" I screamed, trying to break free of Damien's arms.

But Iain didn't seem to hear me. He kept laughing and sending energy bolts around him.
In an instant, his eyes stared into mine. In this brief moment of sanity, he whispered, "Run!"

As soon as he said that, his stare was gone, and he was back to his magic show. The orcs were swarming around him.

"We need to go!" Damien ordered.

Arius and Elashor nodded, but I didn't want to leave Iain.

"Come on!" Elashor pulled on my hand.

Reluctantly, I followed them. We ran through the corridor until we got to a big room at the base of the tower. We closed the door behind us, and I let myself fall to the floor.

Tears started to weep from my eyes. Damien sat on the floor beside me and wrapped his arm around my waist. The contact from his lips to my cheek was warming my heart.

He spoke softly, "Hey, my little wolf. Don't cry."

I sniffled. "But he was our friend."

He replaced a fallen strand of hair, caressing my cheek at the same time.

"I know, but he probably sacrificed himself for us."

I stared at his gray eyes.

"You think so?"

He nodded. "If he didn't die because of the orcs, then he would have died anyway from his wound."

I thought for a minute. He was right. His wound could have been healed if he hadn't pulled at it like he was doing. But the way he opened it, there was no way to heal it.

"Did you see how he was opening his wound? Why would he do that?"

I was angry at Iain. We could have saved him! If only I could have saved him. Guilt crept inside my heart and was eating me up inside.

Damien shrugged.

"He didn't seem to be right in his mind. Maybe some poison from the orc's blade?"

I nodded slowly. "It's possible."

"Maybe he wasn't used to receiving blows and just lost it," suggested Arius.

I looked up at him. Elashor gave me her hand, helping me up.

"He was a mage, after all. They're used to fighting from afar, not being in close battle like that," she suggested.

I shrugged my shoulders. "I guess we'll never know."

I looked around. We were in a big circular room at the base of the tower. Dark stone columns decorated the walls. In the center of the room, the granite tiles formed a star, surrounded by a rose window. At the center of this pattern was a giant black crystal, floating in the air. It seemed to draw power from the top of the tower, and stock it in the ground, or maybe send it somewhere through the ground. I wasn't sure which one.

I took a step forward, but Damien held my hand. "I wouldn't go near it."

I nodded to him. "How the hell are we supposed to destroy this thing?"

Damien smirked and answered, "With this."

He held out a shining orb from under his coat. It looked like a living ball of sun floating in his hand. We all got close to him, staring in awe at the ball of energy.

"What is this?" Elashor whispered.

"Iain gave it to me before we left the castle. It's a concentrated magical bomb."

I stared at Damien in shock. Iain had planned how to destroy this tower all from the beginning. He was saving us twice.

I asked, "Do you think it will be enough to destroy the tower?"

Damien nodded. "Iain said this should be strong enough to blow up the strongest of the buildings. We just need to set it up at the base of the tower. Then we'll have about ten minutes to escape and get the farthest away possible."

"Ten minutes is not enough," commented Arius.

"It is, if there are no enemies chasing us," answered Damien.

The two of them started to argue about if we would make it out in time or not.

I yelled, "It's the only option we have, anyway! The longer we stay here, the more chances orcs are going to come after us."

They stopped arguing and stared at me.

Damien smiled. "You're right, as you always are, my beautiful queen."

I couldn't help but to smile at his words.

Damien put the sphere at the base of the crystal, just at the limit of the energy field that was forming underneath it.

I asked him, "How do you activate it?"

Damien smiled and answered, "Magia, diruptio, inducere, incendo!" He smirked at me and added, "It's activated."

I guess Iain taught him the words, but didn't have time to ask him about it. We had ten minutes to get out of the tower!

"Let's hurry!" shouted Arius before storming out of the room with Elashor. I started running out of the room. Damien followed me.

I bumped into Elashor just as I exited the room. The orcs were back in the corridor, and I wondered where they were coming from, as we had killed so many earlier.

Arius grunted, "We don't have time for this!"

Damien answered, "You're right, then let's not waste time."

Before I could ask him what he meant, two strong arms lifted me into the air. I got my arms behind Damien's neck and landed a kiss on his cheek while we flew over the enemies. Arius followed behind us with Elashor in his arms. Below us, the orcs raged and tried to grab us, but we were too high for them to reach us. In only a few minutes, we were outside the tower, with still a few minutes to spare before the explosion.

The guys didn't stop once we got out, because we had to get as far away from the tower as possible. They kept flying until we heard the sound of crystal shattering. Damien put me back on the ground just in time to turn back and feel the shockwave of the explosion pass through me. We were far enough away that it was just a strong wind, but closer to the tower, the trees lost their leaves.

Damien hugged me from behind and rested his head on my shoulder as we watched the tower explode. Dust was blown from the base of the tower, and the dark crystal shattered as the top of it started to crumble to the floor. Just as the base was almost destroyed, the demons' heads carved into the tower fell to the side and shattered into pieces as they hit the ground, the remaining horns on top of the tower crushed into the forest a little further. The sound of shattering glass mixed with the breaking of wood and leaves rustling. Birds flew away from the sound of the crash. Damien shielded my body from splintering and debris.
When the dust settled, we could see that the tower was no more than a pile of rubbish. More importantly, the thick energy that was bringing us down was gone. There was no more magic attacks on the castle either.

I let out a breath of relief. "I'm so glad that's over!"

Everyone smiled. Arius replied, "Now, all that's left is for Bianca and the others to stop Will."

A knot formed in my stomach. "Do you think they'll succeed?"

He nodded. "I'm sure they will."

Elashor asked, "Shouldn't we join them?"

Damien shook his head. "It would take us days to get to them."

Arius nodded. "Yes, and we don't have the skills to open a portal to get us there."

I wished I could help them, but I had to put my faith in my sister.

"Bianca is, after all, the Moon Goddess's daughter. She should be able to do this."

Damien hugged me as he answered, "I'm sure she will."

Arius was holding Elashor in his arms, looking happier than I've seen him in months.

"We should get back to the castle. The protection spell will wear off soon."

Damien added, "Yes, after this, I think we'll finally get some well-deserved rest."

We had prepared for this war for so long! We had worked tirelessly for years now. I was looking forward to finally resting.

Damien brushed his hand on my cheek. He kissed me gently, his tongue dancing with mine. He whispered to me, "Come, my little wolf. Let us spend the rest of our lives together and get ready for our baby to come."

I smiled as I caressed my tummy. Now, I could finally concentrate on taking care of myself and the baby.

************ Blake's POV ************

Just as I reached the tower, the ground shook. In the sky, the thread of dark energy that was linking the castle to the tower to the south-west was gone. I guess it was a good thing. But I didn't care. I could hear the screams of my sweet Eshenesra coming from the tower.

I tried to open the tower's door, but it was locked. I pushed with my shoulder with all my force, using my full vampiric powers as I did. Pain spread in my shoulder as I did, making me grunt, but I kept on pushing. The wood splintered on my third attempt. Pieces of wood fell through the air as I pushed one last time.

In front of me was a large circular room, full of succubi. To my right was a staircase that hugged the outside of the tower. That's where I needed to go. I could hear Eshenesra coming from up the stairs. But the succubi saw it otherwise. They started attacking me. I was largely outnumbered. More importantly, all the time I spent fighting them was preventing me from saving Eshenesra. Who knew what was going on upstairs?

I fought with two of them, but the others were trying to get at me. I pushed them back with my vampiric force. Then, I summoned a wall, trapping the succubi inside the main room as I got to the stairs. I didn't use my vampiric powers often, but I had to admit it was quite useful.

One of the succubi had managed to get outside the room before I cast the wall spell. I slashed one of her wings off with my sword. Her scream filled the tower. She tried to scratch me with her nails and attack me, but I fought her back. It took a lot of concentration to keep my wall spell on while fighting. The succubus launched herself at me, trying to bite me. I held her at arm's length. Finally, I mustered my strength and dug my sword into her chest, killing her.

A shriek came from the room where Eshenesra was held. I ran up the stairs. I didn't need to stop at all the floors I passed. I could feel through our bond that she was on the last floor.

The door to the main room of the last floor wasn't locked. A putrid smell filled the room. Broken bones and remnants of flesh lingered on the blood-soaked floor. A few succubus statues decorated the room, but most of them were partly destroyed. My sweet Eshenesra was lying unconscious on the floor. Next to her stood what looked like the queen of the succubi. It was a tall woman with a dark bronze-like skin. Her wings were larger than those of the other succubi and she wore black feathers instead of bat wings like the others. She was only wearing a black leather corset; decorated with a bronze cross in front. Her hair was made of fire, blazing through her demon's horns. She stared at me with her fiery eyes.

She hissed at me, "Who dares to disturb my meal?"

I tilted my head left, cracking my neck, rolling my shoulders.

"I'm afraid you won't be eating today."

Her wicked laughter filled the room, resonating through the walls.

"Do you truly think you can stop me, impudent mortal?"

I snickered. "Oh, I've been dead for a long time, demon."

She studied me for a second, then smirked when she realized I was a vampire. "Well, then. We shall see."

She lunged at me, but I kicked her in the chest, knocking her backwards into a statue. The statue exploded into pieces as she fell through. She hissed in frustration and got up, apparently unaffected by my blow.

"You're fucking annoying!" she spat angrily.

Her fiery hair was blazing. She summoned a fire whip, slashing at me with fire. Her whip wrapped around my leather wrist armor. I could feel the heat right through my skin.

I called off icicles on her fire whip, extinguishing the fire. I summoned ice into my blade and swung it at the demon. A white light emanated from it as she countered with a flaming blade. Fire projectiles were projected by the impact of our swords on the ground, narrowly avoiding Eshenesra, igniting the remains of corpses.

Now that the fire had been set to the room, I wanted to end this fight more than ever. Eshenesra was still lying unconscious. I didn't want her to die from asphyxia.

I shouted, "Time for you to die!" As I swung my blade again and again at the demon.
Flame erupted from the demon's body as I lodged the blade into her chest. Her bronze skin was so thick, I only managed to get the tip of the blade in. The demon fought to get the blade out of her chest. I knew I couldn't fail. The life of my mate depended on it.

I grunted as I mustered all the strength that I could, finally getting my sword lodged far into the demon's chest. The demon shrieked from the pain. I knew this wouldn't be enough to kill her, though.

While the demon struggled to remove my blade from her chest, I picked up Eshenesra's body from the floor. Quickly, I flew through the window, hugging her body to mine. I was abandoning my sword to the demon. It was the sword I had been carrying with me ever since I was turned into a vampire. The last remnants of my human life. But it didn't matter. I didn't need it anymore. I was ready to let go of that life I once had. All that mattered now was the woman I held in my arms. With her, I would build a new future full of hopes.

Eshenesra started to stir while we flew. Slowly, she opened her eyes, staring at me.

"Blake?" she whispered. "Where… are… we?"

I tightened my hold on her. "We're going home, my love. I'll make sure that you're healed and then I'll show you how nice the vampire castle is."

She looked around, grabbing my shoulders as she realized we were in the air. "What happened? What about Bianca? And Eurynomos?"

I shushed her softly. "It's okay. Bianca and the others are fighting. They will get to Eurynomos."

She protested, "Don't you think we should help them?"

I frowned. "You almost died in order to break the spell and get them into the castle. You've given enough. It's time that I took care of you."

"But…"

"Enough! You were unconscious for I don't know how long! I almost lost you!"

She stared at me. My heart was hammering in my chest.

I added, with a trembling voice, "Don't you understand just how scared I was of losing you?"

Tears rolled down my cheeks. I couldn't believe it myself. I hadn't cried once since my vampire mother died. I never thought I would find it in me to cry, ever again. But the thought of losing my mate was unbearable.

Eshenesra's warm hand softly wiped the tears off my face.

She smiled warmly, whispering, "You're right, I don't think I can fight at the moment. I need to rest. Please, my love, I can't wait to see my new home."

I landed a soft kiss on her lips, my heart fluttering at her words. For the first time in centuries, I felt happy and peaceful as I flew home, holding the most important woman that ever existed.

Chapter 15 (Bianca)

Reunited

Absolute chaos reigned around me. The sound of cracking skulls and screams filled my ears. I was amazed at how easily I was able to dispose of enemies. The dragons were very effective at dealing with succubi and gargoyles. Zach was fighting simultaneously with his levitating sword and his vampiric powers. I could spot Steven's wolf ripping through enemies. Kõrvits warkots were flying in the air, shooting arrows to enemies on the ground. Slowly, we made our way towards the castle. I couldn't see Blake anymore. The last thing I heard was a scream from Eshenesra, then he was gone. I focused on my main goals: saving my brother and stopping the demon.

I stared at Zach and Steven when we got to the castle's doors. They had the same determination as me in their eyes. We opened the heavy door as the dragons continued fighting enemies outside.

The castle was dark and deserted. The hallway was lit by flames. The sound of our steps echoed as we walked through the hall. We soon came to the throne room, but no one was there. A pedestal of stone seemed to hold a strange portal. Inside, I recognize the place my soul had been held prisoner for some time; the Underworld.

All the rooms that we passed were empty. I knew Will was somewhere inside the castle. We kept walking. Soon, the air started to feel colder. A thin mist escaped my mouth as I breathed. Steven's wolf got closer to me so that I wasn't too cold. I could hear whispers all around us, coming from everywhere and nowhere at the same time. I could make out some words in this chaos of whispers: "Save her," "Traitor," "Killer," "Get out," "Run!"

I looked everywhere, but I couldn't see anything. The whispers grew louder as we got close to a room. I could hear a faint woman's sobbing coming from inside the room. Snow frost and ice crystals formed on the door to this room. All the whispers became one big blur of screams when I put my hand on the frozen doorknob. All the sounds suddenly became silent as I pushed the door open.

The room was freezing, but despite the frost, you could see it was beautifully decorated. A room fit for a queen. I thought. My eyes landed on the bed, where the body of a woman was lying. She was beautiful, her skin still tawny despite the fact her heart wasn't beating anymore. Even though I had never seen her, I knew for a fact this was Leila.

If it wasn't for her blueish lips, you could think that she was only sleeping.

I gasped as I spotted my brother beside her, holding her hand. Or… what used to be my brother. Steven's wolf growled, and Zach took a fighting stance. I watched, disgusted with how my brother's skin was now black and cracked like dried lava. He slowly raised his head, staring at us. His blue eyes were now pitch black. My heart sank when I realized this wasn't my brother anymore. I was facing Eurynomos.

The demon smirked when he saw us. I could feel his disdain as he spoke, "So… You finally made it here. Took you long enough."

This voice didn't belong to my brother. It was a broken, deep, harsh voice.

I shouted at him, rage filling me, "What have you done to my brother?"

His laughter filled the room. Chills ran down my spine.

He spat out with hate, "Oh, but your brother came to me willingly. See, you're too late."

I was trying to sound strong, but my voice trembled, "That can't be!"

The demon smiled. "Yet, here we are."

He sent a wind of energy towards me, making me kneel against my will.

He looked at me with disgust. "You should learn your manners, and bow before your ruler."

I kept my head back and spat back in anger, "I will never bow to you."

I asked him, "What have you done to her?"

He got his attention back to Leila's corpse for a second, then turned back to me.

"Her? Oh, I washed off the blood from her body, and laid her in bed."

I snickered at the demon. "You know very well that's not what I'm asking."

His eyes sparkled as he replied, "I have done nothing more to the dead witch."

"Then why did you bring her to this castle?"

"Oh, I didn't bring her here. Will did. The poor fool wanted to revive her so badly, he agreed to become my vessel. It's a pity I never had any intention to revive the bitch anyway."

As he spoke those words, something moved inside of him, and words were shouted angrily from his mouth with my brother's voice, "You bastard! You lied to me!"

The demon's eyes glared as he screamed, "Shut up!"

A force spread through the demon's body, and my brother disappeared as soon as he had appeared.

I screamed, "You bastard! Release him!"

The demon snickered at me. Lower demons flooded the hallway at the room's entrance, trying to get at us.

Steven pushed through my mind, "Let me get at him."

As the Moon Goddess's daughter, it was my duty to take care of him.

I ordered, "Zach, Steven, take care of the other demons. Eurynomos is mine."

They nodded at me and started to fight the lower demons, pushing them back into the hallway.

I was alone with Eurynomos. He cracked his neck, taking a step towards me.

"I've been waiting for this fight for a long time, bitch. Time to repay for imprisoning me for centuries."

I knew he was talking to the Moon Goddess. I didn't care to say anything back. He launched himself at me, flying through the air. I gasped in pain when his shoulder hit me dead in the chest. I hurled through the air until my back hit the wall, the plaster falling to the floor. He was faster than what I had anticipated.

I got back up. In the blink of an eye, he was beside me and landed an uppercut straight to my jaw. His eyes sparkled with joy as he watched me fly towards the ceiling before landing on my stomach. I swallowed back the bile that rose in my mouth.

A chilling laughter filled the air. "Is that all you can do? I never thought it would be that easy."

I got back up, wincing from the pain. I concentrated on my magic and shot a bolt of lighting towards Eurynomos. He avoided it easily, the lighting bold leaving a black spot on the wall behind him. I turned back just in time to receive a direct hit to my face.

Despair filled me. I needed to find a way to slow him down. The sound of the battle raging outside the room filled the air. Steven and Zach were still busy. I couldn't count on them helping me out for this battle. Strength filled me as I remembered that I was the Moon Goddess's daughter. Eurynomos landed a kick in my stomach. Dust rose in the air as I landed on an old desk, the wood cracking from the weight of my body. I didn't even have time to stand before he was straddling over me, punching me again and again. I was hurting and my head was getting dizzy. If I didn't do anything, he would kill me.

I mustered my strength and pushed him back. I got back up and spat blood on the floor. Eurynomos watched me with disdain. "Where's your beloved Goddess now? Such a coward! Hiding behind a mortal."

My voice trembled despite me. "The Goddess is inside of me."

"You're wrong! She has abandoned you."

"She is my mother. She will never abandon me."

The demon spat on the floor. "Can't you see? She brought you here, so that I could kill you."

Anger built in my chest at those words. I knew he was wrong. The Moon Goddess would never do such a thing.

I snarled at him, "Your soul is damned."

The demon grunted, "Time to die, bitch."

He prepared to launch himself at me again, but I remembered the poison Eshenesra and Blake had given me. I had coated my dagger with it. I threw my dagger at him, hoping it would hit him. He didn't even move or try to avoid it. The dagger stuck in his shoulder. He laughed as he removed the dagger and let it fall to the floor.

"You're going to have to do better than this."

He launched himself at me again, but this time, I was able to avoid him. He tried to kick me, but I jumped in the air and avoided it.

Eurynomos roared in anger. The poison was affecting him, slowing him down. This was exactly what I needed.

He launched himself at me again, but I avoided the attack, and hit him in the face. He hit me in the stomach. I sent a bolt of lightning at him, but he dodged it, leaping into the air and flipping to the wall behind, coming back with a full-force kick to my face. I felt dizzy from the impact, but I kept pushing. I hit him in the face a few times with my fists, imbuing some of the Goddess' magic into them so that they hit harder. Eurynomos recoiled at my punches.

I concentrated as Iain taught me, and as I did, I could see the threads of time materializing all around us. My heart raced as I grasped the power the moon goddess was lending me. Moving through the threads of time allowed me to move faster than Eurynomos. Suddenly, I was able to reappear behind him before he even moved, landing hit after hit to his head. Disbelief showed on his face as I kept beating him despite his best efforts. In one big blast of magic, I sent him flying through the room. He landed in a statue that was lining the wall, shattering it from the impact.

I took a few steps towards him. He was lying down, dizzy. His eyes focused on me, and for a moment, his black eyes were replaced by the deep blues of my brother.

He whispered to me, "Help!"

My heart jumped and I screamed, "Will!"

He rose his dark cracked hand towards me. His lips trembled. "Please… kill me."

My heart shattered at his words. "No! Will, I can't!"

His lips curled up. "You're strong, my dear sister. Please, do it."

His voice was just a murmur. Tears rolled down my cheeks. My brother that I loved so much was asking me to kill him. I didn't know if I had it in me to do this.

I gritted my teeth and clenched my fists as a dark laughter filled the room.

"Are you crying for me?"

His voice was dark, and the blue eyes of my brother were gone. I stared through my teary eyes at the demon. Anger filled me as I realized my brother was trapped in his own body, at the mercy of Eurynomos. As much as it pained me, I knew what needed to be done.

Eurynomos hit me, but I parried each of his hits with mine. As we fought, anger rose inside of me, and as it did, I felt a power filling me. At one point, I was filled with this power. In one big release, I released this energy on him. It was a pure force and came from deep within my soul. Eurynomos fell to the floor, hit by the wrath of the Goddess. He was breathing heavily as he laid on the floor.

I grabbed a sword that laid on the floor nearby as I straddled over his body.

He stared at me with his soulless eyes. "Surely, you wouldn't hurt your own brother, wouldn't you?"

I replied sternly, "My brother is already dead."

I plunged the sword into his heart, pushing the Goddess's energy through it. A white light emanated from the sword, ripping his skin apart. A cry of agony filled the room as his body slowly ripped apart from the Goddess's energy. After a few seconds, the scream was gone, and the demon was dead. I took a step back as white energy spread through the room, all around the demon's body.

At the same moment, Zach and Steven came back into the room, having finally disposed of the lower demons. Steven shifted back to his human form and wrapped me in his arms. We watched in awe as the remnants of the demon's body shook on the floor.

A woman's voice resonated all around us, "Time for you to return to where you belong."

A dark mist seemed to be sucked into the void. A bright, white light appeared beside us, and shaped itself in the form of a beautiful woman. Her hair was blond, almost white, and the air glowed with the light of her golden crown.

She smiled at me. "You have done well, my daughter."

She spread her arms at me, and I ran into her embrace. A wave of emotions came over me. I started to cry, but I wasn't sure why. I just had killed my brother and a demon. I finally met the Goddess who was supposed to be my mother. I was just overwhelmed and let it all flow.

She brushed my hair softly.

"Hush, my child. It's alright. It's over."

She stared at the corpse of what had once been my brother. "Such a pity," she started softly. "He had done so well to help you. Fate has been unfair to him."

She raised her hand towards Will's body, energy drawing from it. A strong wind filled the room. A silhouette started to emerge from the body, and for a while, I was wondering if it was Will, coming back to life. Two huge, black feathered wings sprang from his back as the man rose from the dead body. His once-black hair was now radiant white. Two black horns adorned his head, a reminder of his pact with the demon. A black armor covered most of his body, and he carried two heavy swords. But a pure white energy emanated from him, and his eyes were pure blue. He stood, powerful and pure. He spread his wings, and I realized he had three sets of wings. Two of them were black, the other set of wings was white. He turned to me and smiled.

"You did it, my sister."

I ran into his arms. "Will!"

Tears flowed down my face. He hugged me tightly and kissed the top of my head.

He whispered, "Thank you."

I stepped back as the Moon Goddess motioned to him.

"I have given you eternal life. Your duty will now be to guard Eurynomos, and make sure he stays sealed away, so that something like this may never happen again."

Will bowed his head. "As you wish, my Goddess."

Then she smiled and added, "But you will not be alone."

A white light glowed beside the goddess. A woman appeared in the room. Her skin was tawny, and her eyes were deep brown. She wore a white dress decorated with golden threads. She had a set of white and golden wings and carried a golden scepter. Will's eyes sparkled when he saw her, his mouth wide open.

She ran into his arms. He embraced her, lifting her in the air as their mouths crushed together. Tears rolled down their cheeks as they kissed. When they finally let go, he whispered to her, "I can't believe you're finally in my arms again."

The Moon Goddess smiled. "Together, you will watch that Eurynomos stays sealed for eternity."

They both nodded to the Goddess. She opened a portal for them. Will laced his fingers with Leila, looking at her like she was the most beloved treasure in the world.

They both waved at us as they walked peacefully into the portal, where they would stay for eternity. I was sad to see my brother leave, but relieved he got his mate back. I knew he would keep us safe. I had faith in him. Eurynomos would stay sealed.

The Goddess gestured to us, then faded away from the room.

Steven's arms wrapped around me as reality set back in. It was over. The demon was defeated.

"Let us return home," I said to Zach and Steven.

They nodded, and we started walking out of the castle. The demon's army was either all lying dead or had fled back to the Underworld.

As we got into the courtyard, the dragons were all standing, waiting for us. Cara and Ladon took a step towards us as we got out. They nodded at us, and even though I couldn't communicate with them, I could understand the gratitude they felt. Their masters were reunited and could love each other for eternity.

The dragons nodded to us and flew away together towards the west. I guess their task was done. They were now free to do whatever they wanted.

Steven pushed through my mind, "Now that the demon's dead, does this mean I'll finally get to mark you as my mate?"

I smirked at him. I didn't need to answer. His wolf understood and purred in his chest.

"Let's get home," I said out loud.

Steven added, "Hey Zach, do you mind flying with Bianca? We'll get back faster if I run as a wolf, and you fly."

Zach smirked at him. "Well, you're quite eager to get home, aren't you?"

Steven laughed at his question. "I have business waiting for me."

I could feel his need for me through our mate bond. He had been waiting for this for years now. He didn't wait for an answer and changed into his wolf form. Zach grabbed me in his arms, and we flew in the direction of the vampire's castle. I grabbed onto Zach as I watched Steven's wolf run beneath us.

Epilogue (Bianca)

A New Hope

The tiny prince slept in my arms as I rocked him. He had his father's brown hair and his mother's hazel eyes. The first werewolf-vampire hybrid to be born. Or if one was born one day, history had forgotten him. Ancient legends spoke of how powerful hybrids were. Would he be a kind ruler? All I knew was that this child was loved by every member of his family, whether vampire or werewolf. Kate was a wonderful mother, and Damien was proud and keen to show him how to be a good ruler.

I smiled as my thoughts drifted to Steven. I had finally let him mark me, giving in to his wolf's desires. It was a few months ago, yet the memories of it were still as delicious as they were then. When we got back to the pack, after killing Eurynomos, we discovered that Jane had left the pack after Will broke up with her, never to return. The pack had been left alone and unprotected. We told them that Will had died without speaking of the deal he had made with the demon. The pack was happy to see us, and gladly accepted me as their Luna, and my mate as their Alpha. After all, I was the former Alpha's daughter.

We came for a vacation to the castle as soon as we heard Kate and Damien had their baby. I knew this baby would make a fine prince. I wished Will and Leila could have met him. Although I knew his uncle would always watch over him.

Just as I thought about that, a light sparked outside, and two sparrows landed on the edge of the window. I smiled. That's right, his aunt was watching over him too, at her mate's side. The two sparrows flew inside the room, signing a joyous melody before flying back out in the warm spring morning.

I rocked the baby to sleep, humming an elven song that Elashor had taught me. A song about a great hero and his loving mate. One is a dark, fallen angel; the other sacrificed herself, pure as light. Together, they keep the demon at bay, so that the world of the livings can be at peace.

Hi,

I really hope you enjoyed The Fallen. Please don't forget to leave a review on Amazon and Goodreads. Reviews are the best way to support authors.

What happens to this young prince? Check out what destiny awaits him in the Award-Winning Best Seller Cursed King.

https://www.amazon.com/dp/B0CCYWGL5D

Want to know more about the origins of Leila's pack? Delve into an ancient world full of love, lust, deception, and death. Discover the truth about the people who were called the Goddess's Wards.

Grab your copy now on Amazon!

https://www.amazon.com/dp/B0BPRGP9L7

Don't forget to subscribe to my mailing list! And if you feel like it, go on my website, and drop me an email. I'd love to learn more about you! What do you like? What's your favorite trope? What do you despise?

Thank you for your love and support,

Danielle Paquette-Harvey

daniellephauthor.com

Acknowledgments

I can't believe this is the end of my first series! What an unbelievable ride this has been! Thanks to everyone who believed in me.

Of course, I want to thank my husband, Martin, and my kids for their love and encouragement. You guys are amazing and I'm so happy to have you in my life! I can't imagine my life without you.

I want to thank my soul triplets. You guys are amazing, and your love and support means the world to me. I love you with all my heart.

Thanks to all my close friends! The ones I knew before becoming an author, and the ones I made since I've become an author. Yes, virtual friends count as much as friends that live nearby. You guys have become a part of my life. I speak to some of you daily. I hope one day I get to visit each of you!

Life is crazy! We all are busy, but I hope we'll never be too busy for each other. Love is what keeps us strong.

Love you guys! See you soon.

Danielle